Going Offside

Van Cole

Published by Van Cole, 2023.

GOING OFFSIDE

First edition. August 9, 2023.

ISBN: 979-8215969632

Written by Van Cole.

Going Offside
Gay Enemies to Lovers Romance

By: Van Cole

By: Van Cole

Foreword

A childhood friend turns into a college rival, and the worst thing is I want him, badly.

We were preparing for the big football game against our rivals when I saw him, my old childhood friend. Now he's strutting his stuff as a male cheerleader, his tight muscles on display, playing havoc with my mind.

I've still been struggling to come out. The last thing I need is to have a crush on a rival cheerleader, especially when that person is from my past. I have to try and keep things a secret because there's no way an enemy can become a lover, but why can't I stop thinking about him? Is this just a case of opposites attracting?

I have to try and keep it together because if anyone finds out then my cover will be blown and I'm not ready to be out. My Dad would kill me. But damn if I don't hate the way Liam makes it look so easy...

Going Offside

Chapter One

Finn

"Alright guys, you know what time it is. It's the biggest game of the season. Sure, some of you might think this life is all about winning trophies, but those fade into memory. It's all about taking everything you have onto that field and making sure that you leave nothing behind, especially when it comes to your rivals. The Cavaliers are on a winning streak. You've all seen the humiliation. You've grown up with it. Do you think you're the team to break that? Because I sure do. I don't need to tell you what it's like when you drive around with your proud Eagle jackets on only to be hollered at by those jerks on the other side of the city. I've heard all the taunts. They should be echoing in your mind right now because I want you to think of them when you step out onto that field. I want you to see them laughing at you, because that's exactly what they're doing. Do you know what their coach is saying to them now? He's telling them that the game is already won. He's saying that he doesn't even need to give a team talk because we're going to crumble under the weight of pressure, just like all the other teams have before us. Well, I say no! I say that we are going to make a stand and this is the year when their streak is going to end. Winning a trophy this season isn't going to mean shit if you don't beat them because they're just going to hold that win over you all your lives. Every time you go to a job interview, every time you go on a date, every time anyone sees you in the street, they're always going to see a failure, and I do not want that for you, so what are you going to do?"

"Win!"

"What are you going to do?!"

"WIN!"

"Tell me what the hell you're going to do!"

"WIIINNNNNN."

The chorus echoed around me and through me, as though the sound had taken on a life of its own. It filled up the locker room and made the air thick with tension. We stamped our feet against the floor, creating an even greater noise. Coach Jackson's face was twisted with anger. He had been brought in precisely to break this streak. Year after year we had laid down and let the Cavaliers take a huge dump right on our chests, and this was the year when it was all going to change.

I had been there the previous year as backup. I hadn't even made it onto the field. I'd seen the effect it had on the team though. They had walked out there looking as though they were already beaten, and afterwards they were on the verge of tears. I never wanted that for me. I knew that coach was right. Maybe some people would think it was a myth, but there was a sharp correlation between those who lost as Eagles and those who failed in life. The Cavaliers, well, they went on to great success. Failure bred failure and at some point, it had to end. We were all hoping that we wouldn't get tainted with the same brush.

"Now I want you to watch this. Study it like you've never studied it before. They're fast, they're good, and they're going to hammer you. They're not going to stop until you're a beaten, bloodied pulp, so you have to stand tall and make sure they know that you're not beaten. If you do that then maybe you stand a chance of winning. It starts in the heart first, but you have to be smart about it as well. Watch these plays. Learn how they think. You might think it's cheap to want to be like them, but they're winners. They've proven themselves. If there's anything we can learn from them then we have to use it. I don't want your eyes to leave this screen," Coach Jackson said, as his assistant wheeled the TV in and set it up.

The picture flickered into life and a hush fell over the locker room. I swept a stray lock of dark hair away from my face. Nerves were already running through my veins. I glanced around, wondering if anyone else was feeling the same way I was. The last thing I needed was to let the pressure get to me, but with every year that passed so did the burden get placed on the shoulders of another team, and by now the weight of the entire school was upon us. I should have been brave, but I couldn't quite make it there yet.

I watched as the Cavaliers tore through teams time and time again. They were quick, strong, and ruthless. In some ways it was as though they were the perfect football team, as though they had been forged in some lab somewhere. Suddenly the picture jerked and something caught my eye. In the lower corner the cheerleaders were there. Three of them were bouncy, perky blondes with petite frames and the kind of smiles that made most men melt. But they weren't what I was looking at. I saw him, a tall, slender man wearing skin tight clothes that showed off every chiseled muscle. His buttocks were tight and the outline of his manhood was on display. Apparently, he didn't know what shyness was. He jumped as high as the girls and the elegance of his body was something to be admired. He was graceful and he exuded the kind of sex appeal that sent my heart into overdrive. The pom poms obscured his face, but I was already transfixed. I had never seen anything like it before, and I could just tell that he was gay.

I shifted uncomfortably in my seat, and lowered my head, although I could not tear my gaze away from him. I was afraid that someone would notice what I was looking at. My skin felt warm. If they should ever find out... no, it didn't even bear thinking about. Tension gripped my heart and suddenly I found it difficult to breathe. Had the temperature increased? Sweat prickled on my brow and my mouth was suddenly dry.

The cheerleader didn't suffer from those effects though. He was out there, proud and defiant, unafraid of what the world thought of him. How I wished that I could be like that. I envied people like him, for I was still deeply in the closet. But more than that, I desired him. His body was perfect, his muscles were defined, but it was his confidence that left me reeling. Arousal stirred within me and I felt a twitch. I crossed my legs, tensing my muscles in other areas to stop the erection before it fully took hold. The last thing I wanted was for someone to see me getting hard. I felt like I was a teenager again.

The coach was still going on about the last play. I knew I should be listening, but I just couldn't take my attention off the cheerleader. It was as though he was magic. At some point he jumped high in the air and split his legs. I marveled at the flexibility and all that it promised. The girls flipped and bounced around him, but they were nothing compared to him. He was the star of the show and he knew it, for sure. The pom poms fell and were caught, and then he turned to face the camera. At that point I gasped, and Coach Jackson had moved onto the next clip.

It wasn't anything that I could have been prepared for, and the sight of him had struck my heart, for I knew him. His name was Liam and we had been childhood friends, next door neighbors in fact. We used to spend every day together until his parents moved away. He always promised he would write, but he never did. I always thought he had been a good friend to me, but he had proven that he was just the same as any other person. There was nothing special between us, nothing that could have lasted. He had always been able to make friends far more easily than me, I guess he found it easy to forget me. I had always resented him for that. Sometimes I thought that if I could have had one friend to confide in then I might have been a different person. I could have been as flamboyant and as confident as he was. As I watched him in that video, he looked the complete opposite to me. I was in a shell, forced to hide my true feelings and my real self. Liam could be whoever he wanted to be. He had left me, escaping the neighborhood, finding a more liberal home. Maybe it wasn't fair to him that I should have been so envious, but I just couldn't help thinking that he had all the luck. My blood burned and I was filled with mixed feelings, and anger replaced my arousal.

Now he was at the rival school and I was going to have to see him again. Suddenly the game just got a hell of a lot more complicated.

Was he going to remember me? Was I going to let him know that I remembered him?

I couldn't believe that I had actually thought of him in that way. I tried to swallow the awkward feelings inside, but they just wouldn't go away. I put my head in my hands and tried to pretend that this had never happened.

"What's wrong Finn? Are you starting to freak out? Because if you are then you can get right out. I need men whose heads are in the game," Coach Jackson said. Suddenly all eyes were on me.

"I'm not freaking out coach. I'm just picturing how I'm going to push their faces in the dirt," I shot back, trying to sound as angry as I could.

Coach smirked. "That's what I like to hear. I want every one of you to be like Finn, you hear me? This is a war. I want you to leave blood on that field."

I gulped and held my bag over my lap, embarrassed at the way I had reacted. Now that I had seen Liam, I couldn't get him out of my mind. The way he moved, the way he... oh God. I had to get home as quickly as possible.

*

I was sitting at the dinner table with the folks. They had insisted that I stay at home to save money on accommodation, instead of getting the full college experience. They said it was better this way, because it meant I could focus on my studies and not get distracted by anything that wasn't important. Apparently, the word 'fun' didn't exist in any of the dictionaries my Dad owned. I still hadn't been able to stop thinking about Liam, although I had gotten my feelings under control after taking a shower when I got home. I felt a little dirty because of it though.

"Hey Dad, do you remember our old neighbors, they had that son Liam?" I asked.

Dad scowled immediately and gripped his cutlery tightly, as though they were weapons.

"What about them?" he asked, spitting the words as though they were venom. I was taken aback by the force of his voice. I hadn't realized it had been such a sore point for him.

"I just thought that I saw Liam in one of the videos Coach showed us for the next game. I think he might be a cheerleader."

"Figures," Dad said, glowering. "I always knew there was something off about that kid. There was something off about them too. I don't know what was going through their minds, all that liberal crap. It's no wonder he turned out the way he did. I can't imagine how embarrassed I would be if you were prancing up there as a cheerleader. The world has gone mad. What's wrong with things just being the same? Girls are cheerleaders and guys play football. It's as simple as that," he said, shaking his head as though that was the only determination that anyone needed. A part of me wanted to challenge him, but I had made that mistake before. Dad was one of those people who weren't interested in having a rational debate. He knew what he knew and he liked the world to be the way he wanted it to be. There was nothing to do about it but nod and accept that that was the way he felt. It didn't help me any though. I had always dreamed of coming out to my parents. I'd watched a lot of people who spoke about their situations and most of them said that it wasn't as bad as they had feared.

Most of them didn't have my father though. Mom wasn't so bad, although she never actively spoke out against Dad. She would just shrug and smile and then try to move on. I could imagine what would happen if I tried to come out. Dad would rant and rave and wonder where I had gone wrong. He'd try to look for a solution, as though being gay was something that could be fixed rather than just a part of me. I quickly grew envious of Liam. He lived a life where he could be out and proud and open with his sexuality. Soon enough we would meet again after so many years. I wonder if he would remember me. I wonder if he had any advice.

I was almost afraid of seeing him again though, because if Dad saw me then he would kill me. After dinner I went back to my room and snuggled under the covers. Despite myself I couldn't stop thinking about the way Liam looked in that tight cheerleading outfit. I hated myself for thinking about him like this because deep down I was angry with him. He could have stayed in touch. He could have been my friend instead of just casting me aside. I found myself wishing that I could have been more like him. In another life we could have been friends, but now we were opposites and we were enemies, but even so I closed my eyes and lost myself to the sweet fantasy, pretending for just a moment that I didn't have to be afraid of being gay, pretending that I could live another life.

Chapter Two

Liam

The college was alive with spirit. I found it infectious. It was like a drug that was injected straight into my veins. I couldn't get enough of it. Sweat flecked my brow and trickled uncomfortably under my tight training gear, but it was almost over. The world spun as I did a backflip and felt the thump of my landing reverberate up my legs. I held myself in position and then allowed myself to relax. There was a smattering of applause from Linda, Tess, and Bailey. I high fived them as I grabbed a towel and ran it around my face and neck, wiping the sheen of sweat away.

"We're going to dazzle them!" Linda said,

"Hell yeah, they're not going to know what hit them," I replied.

"They might think this is all about the football game, but it's not. It's more than that," Tess said.

"I wish you could teach me how to flip like that," Bailey said. The grunting sounds of people working out was a cacophony in the gym, while outside the football team was practicing. We always tried to keep our practices at the same time to create a kind of unity between the cheerleaders and the football players, although it didn't always work. They were the stars of the show of course, and hated anyone trying to take attention away from them, something that we were particularly good at.

"I think we need a good victory routine this year. We really need to hammer it home to them that they're second best. The football team might humiliate them with the score, but we need to make sure they never forget that they're losers," Linda said. She was vicious. You wouldn't think it to look at her, what with her angelic look, her ruby lips and her blonde hair that was tied in pigtails. Her blue eyes sparkled with a frenzy though and she never took prisoners lightly. Tess was dark skinned, with eyes like chocolate and straight black hair that was the color of midnight. Bailey was chirpy and petite, with auburn hair that curled to the middle of her back. I was the odd one out, as I was most places I went. I didn't mind though. I had gotten used to it over the years. Being the only male cheerleader in the whole damn region was something that some people would have been ashamed of, but not me.

I ran my hand through my dark hair and arched an eyebrow at Linda.

"Are you sure you really want to be that cruel?" I asked.

"Hell yes," she said, and then laughed. The three of them cackled like witches.

"I just want to do something to catch Bobby's attention. I need some real big flourish or something," Bailey said. The other two girls rolled their eyes towards me. I sighed a little. They had grown impatient with Bailey's crush, so it was up to me to take things into my own hands.

"Bailey, don't you think you should focus your attention on someone who actually wants to spend time with you?" I asked.

Bailey frowned. "You just don't understand. He does want to spend time with me, he just doesn't know it himself yet. All I need to do is make him see. He just hasn't made the effort yet. Once he sees me then he'll understand that I'm the only girl for him. Besides, it's not like he's going out with anyone else. He's waiting for someone special, and that someone is me. I just have to prove it to him," she stuck up her nose as though she was a princess. The girl liked a challenge, I'll give her that. This one might have been impossible though.

"I just think-"

"I don't care what you think Liam. The fact is that you're all supposed to be my friends and I would appreciate a little support in this matter. Is that too much to ask?"

I glanced at the other two and we sighed. "Fine Bailey, have it your way. I do genuinely hope that you get what you want. I just don't want you to miss out on any other opportunities while you're waiting for something that might never happen."

"There's no point in being with anyone other than Bobby. He's my soul mate," she said, folding her arms across her chest. I averted my gaze from her. Things with Bobby were... complicated. His parents had led a committee to ban me from being a cheerleader, saying that it went against the spirit of the college or something like that. It was a load of crap, just the same kind of thing I'd been dealing with all my life where people don't seem to want me to be a part of anything just because I'm different. Thankfully we live in a time where being gay is a little more acceptable, and their complaints were summarily dismissed.

"Speaking of soul mates, how are things with Hank?" I asked Tess, who gave me a face that said I should never have asked.

"Let's just say that I'm not welcome at his folk's place for a little while," Tess said. There was a lot of hurt emotion behind her words, and I think I can understand where it came from.

"Well, my love life is going just swimmingly," Linda said.

"I bet it is for you, not for his wife," Bailey said. Linda wasn't the only vicious one. She didn't seem to mind though. In fact, she wore the fact that she was having an affair with a married man as a badge of pride. She wouldn't say who it was, although the rest of us thought that it was a professor at college. We just couldn't pin down who.

After we finished stretching, we went back to the locker rooms, although this was where we parted. Despite being a cheerleader, I was still a man, so I had to be sent back into the sweaty, heavy, pungent male locker room. Before we left though, Tess pulled me back. She ran a hand through her hair and looked pensive.

"Can I talk to you about something?" she asked.

"This about Hank?" I replied.

She nodded.

"What exactly happened between you two?" I asked.

She rolled her eyes and sighed. "It was a stupid thing. We'd been getting a little ahead of ourselves and we were joking around about the future, even about kids and stuff. It's not like we were actually planning to do anything like that, we were just talking. Anyway, his folks overhead us and later that night his mom thought I was asleep. She was speaking to Hank outside the door in a whisper and she had this conversation with him where she..." Tess closed her eyes and formed a fist with her hand, bumping it against her forehead, "she told him that he might want to think about his options before he commits to having a kid that's going to be... different," she said the word with the same sort of spite that I imagined Hank's mom said it with.

"That's just what you want to hear. Why is everyone so afraid of being different? What did Hank say?"

She shrugged. "He doesn't really get what the big deal is and why I'm so upset. He says that she didn't mean anything by it, but it does mean something and I can't just pretend to forget it. Like, what, I'm good enough to date her son but she only wants a white grandchild? I don't know, I guess I hoped he'd be a little angrier on my behalf. Anyway, I just wanted to ask you... have you ever been in a situation like this? Have parents ever gotten in your way?"

I snorted with laughter. "Only once, because I learned a long time ago to never let it get to the stage where parents can interfere. There was this guy I liked, you know, I was pretty young so it wasn't romantic or anything, but we were good friends. I always thought there was something there even before I knew what that something could be. I moved away and sent him some letters. He never replied. I don't think it was him though, I think it was his dad. He had a real hard on for trying to control people. I guess he figured I was gay and didn't want me getting anywhere near his son."

"That sucks."

"Yeah, but look, all I'll say is that parents can get on with their own lives. They're always going to have problems or find it hard to deal with something. It's just the way parents are. God forbid that we should become like that when we get older," I pulled a face, and this made Tess laugh. "What you really have to watch out for is Hank's reaction. If he's not going to stand up for you then to me that raises a red flag. You don't want to have to be fighting this battle alone, and if he's not standing up for you now then can you guarantee that he's going to stand up for your kid?"

The skin in between her eyebrows crinkled with thoughts, and she nodded. "I think I'm going to have to have a talk with him tonight. Great. That's the last thing he's going to want to do. By the way, when are you going to tell Bailey that you had a thing with Bobby?"

"How about this side of never? It would kill her," I said.

Tess sighed. "Secrets never do anyone any good," she said, and walked on to her changing room.

She might well have been right, but revealing secrets never seemed to do much good either. That was the other complication with Bobby; we'd had a little flourish of a romance. It was just a bit of fun, a fumble after getting drunk at a party. Unfortunately, he had the same attitude as his parents and so he was at the point where he loathed himself. If I wanted a project then I could have tried to coax the confidence out of him, but I have neither the time nor the energy for that. I can't deal with people who don't know themselves. I want someone who can be utterly free with me, and who I can be free with. I'm not going to skulk around and counsel someone through their anguish. Life is too short for that.

But speaking about the past did bring Finn to mind. I hadn't thought about him for a while. It shouldn't have still stung, but it did. We were good friends. We used to spend all our time together. In fact, he was even my first kiss. It was a stupid little thing. We were behind his bedroom door and I guess we wanted to practice what we had seen adults do on TV. It never seemed wrong that we were two boys. I don't know if he remembered or not. I don't even know if it counts as a proper first kiss, but that was that. Then I moved away and I thought I would try keeping in touch. We said we would write to each other, and then nothing.

I guess that's the way it goes in life and love though; most of the time you end up with a whole load of nothing.

*

I walked into the locker room. As soon as I opened the door I was hit with the stench of these men. I went to my locker and pulled out a towel and a change of clothes. They had gotten accustomed to my presence now, although some of them still wrapped their towels around their waists or angled their bodies away from me while they were showering so that I couldn't betray their modesty. Not that I cared anyway, there was nothing particularly sexy about seeing these Neanderthals scrub themselves clean after a sweaty practice. It didn't help that none of them were particularly refined and it was clear they had no interest in me. I wasn't about to pursue a lost cause.

I caught Bobby glaring at me though, and just smiled at him in reply. This infuriated him even more and he slammed his locker shut. He'd better be careful, because all that pent up anger was going to burst a blood vessel at some point. Life was much easier for everyone if you could just accept who you were. I'd done so a long time ago and I was laughing. Sure, people glared at me or insulted me or spat at me, and I'd been threatened far too many times for my liking, but at least I didn't have to go home every night and wonder how I could have pretended to be someone else.

It's why I liked Linda, Tess, and Bailey. At least they knew who they were. We could all be honest about our faults.

As I got changed, I heard a few of them talk about the upcoming game with our big rivals. If things had gone differently then I could have been in the other locker room, which was no doubt drenched in misery as they had been on one of the biggest losing streaks in history.

Our team was confident of extending the streak though, which was why we wanted to figure out a routine that would mark the occasion. As they spoke, I heard a few of the opposing players mentioned and one name caught my ear; Finn.

It seemed as though we were going to have a long-awaited reunion. A smile curled on my lips as I thought about the look on his face when his team got thrashed by us. I'd wave my peach of an ass in his face, and it would be even better if his father was in attendance. I'd show them all how glorious it was to be gay, and how nobody should ever be shunned.

Chapter Three

Finn

I still hadn't been able to think straight after I had seen the man Liam had turned into. Most of my childhood was a blur of a memory, almost as though I was watching someone else's life, but his friendship was one of the anchors of my mind. I couldn't believe that he could just let it end like that, that he could just move away and begin a new life. The more I thought about it the angrier I got. I had been neglected in so many different ways, by so many different people, and I started to think it had all begun with Liam. If he hadn't turned his back on me then I would have been more confident. Maybe I would have been able to be honest with myself and come out. I would have been a different person, a better person, but I wasn't. Because of him.

Well, I would soon make him pay. I would make all of them pay. I was going to charge down the field and make sure that we took our pride back. This game wasn't just for points or a league standing. This was for something far more powerful and more ethereal than that. If we lost this, we would be letting the entire city down, at least the half that supported us.

It was late at night and I was out back, practicing throwing, catching, and sprints. Dad came out, holding a beer. He may not have been the perfect father, but he had always spent time with me. For hours in the evening, he threw the ball with me, and now it was paying dividends. It wasn't quite the same now though. Instead of a ball in his hand it was usually a beer, although he was still eager to offer any criticisms. Like now, when he told me that I was angling my body wrong.

I went through a few more motions before I gave up for the night. He grabbed me a bottle of water from the cooler and gestured for me to take a seat on one of the loungers beside him. I sipped the water. I would have been envious of the beer if I had liked it. Sweat trickled down the sides of my face. The evening was balmy, with red streaks slashing across the purple sky. The sun was dipping below the horizon, ending another day.

"I wanted to say that I'm proud of you son," Dad began. It was rare that we should ever have a heart-to-heart conversation like this. He had never taught me to shave, or about the birds and the bees (frankly I was glad that I had missed out on the latter).

"Thanks Dad," I said, I was tempted to ask why, but he wasn't going to keep it a secret.

"A lot of men lose their way when they get to your age. They discover women and booze," he glanced at his beer as he said this, "and they start to lose their discipline. The folly of youth has always prevented some men from being great, and I just wanted to say that I'm proud of you for not going down that path."

"Thanks... I think."

"No, I'm serious. I've always tried to give you a strict work ethic, but with kids you can never be sure how they're going to pan out. You stuck to yours though. You're putting the work in and I know it's going to pay off. While other people are frittering their time away on relationships that aren't going to last and drunk nights they're never going to remember, you're putting the hard yards in. Let me tell you that when all is said and done, you're going to be the one they envy. You're going to be the one who has it all. I know this is a big game, and I have every faith that you're going to be able to pull it off. This is the year the streak ends. You're the man to bring pride back to us," he said.

I said thanks again, and then made an excuse to leave, saying that I needed a shower. I didn't need that kind of pressure, but I also didn't need him giving me this false praise. There was a reason why I hadn't distracted myself with any of these things, and it wasn't because I was a straight edge or dedicated to my craft.

It was just because I was scared.

The truth is that I craved companionship, but I could never allow myself to actually have it because what was the point? I'd never actually be able to have a relationship, and the thought of having a one-night stand with someone... well... I wouldn't know where to begin. And if I got drunk, I'd be afraid that I might say something out of turn and suddenly my secret would be out. It might not be the end of the world for some people, but I know my parents would disown me. Dad had spoken a lot about having grandchildren and I didn't want to disappoint him. He'd only be angry with me, so it was better to just put that part of my life to the side and hope that one day when I was living somewhere else, I could indulge myself.

It might be a long wait though, and I groaned at the thought that I might have to be condemned to solitude for a long time.

I doubted Liam had that problem. He was out there, strutting before the football team, stealing the spotlight from the other cheerleaders. He probably had a string of men waiting for his call, and nobody was going to tell him that he couldn't be gay. I wished I possessed his self confidence.

I wished I was him.

If I could just have an ounce of it, just enough to take a risk then maybe I could feel better about myself. If I just had the strength to tell Dad how I felt and explain that this wasn't a choice I was making... but I didn't have it. I was just going to have to drift through life and hope that eventually something would make things better

*

I had been invited back to Matt's dorm. He was in my class and on the football team, so we got on pretty well. Like everyone else I had kept him at arm's length though, afraid that if anyone got to know me too well, they would also see my secret. I always liked being invited to the dorms though. It gave me a sense of what the college experience should really be like. When I decided to stay near home my parents said I should stay with them because it would save a lot of money. It seemed to make sense then, but I hadn't realized how much I would be missing out on by doing so. Matt had posters of other football players on his wall. His roommate was out. We were sitting with our backs against the wall on Matt's bed, with books open in front of us. Matt had dreamy eyes and sandy hair. He didn't have a girlfriend, which surprised me, and I found that I couldn't stop looking at him. I tried to not get crushes on people I played football with because it only made things more complicated, but with guys like Matt it was impossible.

"I really can't concentrate on this," he said, throwing his hands up in the air.

"It's the game, isn't it?" I asked.

Matt nodded. "I keep trying to tell myself that it's not really too much of a big deal and it's only one game, but it is a big deal and it's not just one game. I can't get it out of my head though. I keep imagining that I'm going to end up costing us big. I know Coach is trying to get us all aggressive and everything, but it's making me tense."

"I know, sometimes I wish he'd ease up a little bit. I guess he was brought back for this game in particular. If we don't break this curse soon then I guess there's a sense that we're never going to."

"Do you think it really is a curse?" Matt asked. I tilted my head, as though I didn't quite understand the question. It was more a figure of speech than anything else. "You know," Matt elaborated, "the thing Coach said about how the people who have lost over the years have ended up being failures in life as well?"

"I guess it sticks in the mind, doesn't it? If you keep getting told you're a failure then you're going to start believing it, and then it doesn't matter what you're going to do," I said.

Matt nodded thoughtfully. "I don't want to be a failure. It's bad enough that I'm already a disappointment in my dad's eyes."

"Why?" I asked, furrowing my brow with concern. I couldn't imagine anyone being disappointed with him.

Matt sighed and stroked his hand through his sandy hair. It was thick and it looked soft. I found myself having to wrench my gaze away, because I was beginning to wonder what it would be like to feel that myself.

"I don't know if you know, but I was dating this girl called Sarah and things were pretty serious for a while. We were talking about marriage and the future, and Dad wanted me to get all my ducks in a row. Anyway, then it didn't work out. Dad got angry. He blamed me for it, and he kept telling me that sometimes in life we have to work through things even when they're not easy, because those are the things that mean the most. I was trying to tell him that we weren't happy together anymore, but he wouldn't listen."

"Is that really why things ended?" I asked.

Matt nodded. "It was just with college, you know, you get exposed to different things and I guess you want different. I think we both felt as though we were holding each other back. But then look at me now, it's not exactly like I'm setting the world alight without her. I don't know... it's just complicated. I wish someone could sit down and tell me what a relationship should be like and how I should act when I'm in one. It's all too difficult. What about you? Do you have anyone?"

"No," I said, trying my hardest not to blush. "I decided that I was going to focus on my studies and try and wait for all of that after college."

"Smart guy," Matt said, spreading out his arms, "maybe I should have the same outlook. I keep thinking that college is the one time in our lives when we're free to do whatever we want without the world judging us for it. You know, we can just let ourselves go without feeling any guilt or anything, and sometimes I think I should just do it, I should just do everything I can while I have the chance because what if I end up getting older and I just regret it all?"

I wasn't sure if I was reading the signals correctly, but he had shifted his body position to where there was less distance between us. I could feel the heat radiating off his body. The things he was saying spoke to my mind. I wanted to be able to explore as well and I wished there hadn't been such a risk with it. Perhaps Matt was telling me that he wanted to feel something different. Maybe the reason why things hadn't worked out with Sarah was because he needed a man's touch. My throat went tight and tension filled my body, but I began to think that if I wasn't going to take advantage of these opportunities then I was never going to find anyone.

He was practically begging me to touch him. The air was heavy with the scent of his aftershave and my mind was heady with desire. I thought about what Liam might do in the same situation, and knew that he would have no reservations. It was time for me to be more like Liam. It was time for me to take my life into my own hands. We were already feeling the pressure of the game. Maybe this was exactly what we needed. My head was filled with thoughts of romance, of a love blossoming between two football players.

It took everything I had, but I summoned my courage and bravery and began to reach out towards him. My fingers brushed his and for a moment my body was alive with the sheer thrill of crackling electricity. Heat blazed within me and I turned to him, expecting to see the same look of desire in his eyes, but instead there was disgust. He pulled his hand away and recoiled, looking at me as though I was insane.

I was mortified.

I pushed myself off the bed and stammered out an apology. I don't remember what I said because I was too flustered. All I wanted was to get out of there and pretend that none of it had happened. I wished I had never gone there in the first place, and I prayed to God that he wouldn't tell anyone.

Chapter Four

Liam

It was the evening of the big game. Because we were in the same city, we didn't need to travel on a coach anywhere the night before, so we were just in our usual haunt. The football players were usually spending time together partying, although never too hard because the Coach ran them pretty ragged. The night before a game there was a curfew, although nobody bothered to obey it, especially not before this one. They were believing the game was already won, which I thought was a mistake, but I wasn't about to tell them that. It didn't seem to matter that there was a different team every year; the end result was the same. Maybe I was worrying too much about this one.

Maybe I was preoccupied thinking about Finn.

The girls and I had our own pre-match ritual. We'd get together and watch a movie, have a few drinks, and stay up late. It didn't matter as much if we were a little hungover, although in our eyes our performance was just as important as the players. If we failed in our role then the whole school spirit was going to be fading, and if the team was losing, we wouldn't be able to bring them up again.

Tonight was a strange night though. Linda was angsty and she kept checking her phone. In the end she said that she had to leave. I guess her married man had a hot date, although they were always at the strangest hours of the night so I didn't think he was taking her out to some fancy restaurant. What could we say to her though? She had convinced herself that this was some great romance.

Bailey was checking her phone as well. I had peeked at her messages once, just a glimpse over the shoulder, and it was depressing. There was a string of messages she had sent Bobby, interspersed with a few replies that he had given her. It was as though she was starving and he was giving her crumbs, just enough to keep her on the hook without ever giving her enough to fully nourish her. I wasn't sure if he was doing this out of malice or just because he wanted to keep a girl around in case he needed some ass , but it wasn't cool. Bailey was the only one suffering. Maybe I was a coward for not telling her the truth straight out, but even if she heard that Bobby was gay, I doubt it would deter her. She probably thought she could switch him back.

Tess was despondent as well. I guessed she was still pretty broken up about what had happened between her and Hank. Maybe he hadn't stepped up like a good man should have. I doubted she told Linda and Bailey. Neither of them knew what it was like to be different, to always feel the glare of other people even when they thought they were not staring. It was left for me to be the life of the party, but the party didn't last very long. Linda's phone finally vibrated and she jumped up, racing out barely saying goodbye, and then Bailey said that she was going to try and find Bobby. She had some theory that before a big game he was more likely to want to get laid, so she was going to try and strike while the iron was hot. That left me and Tess alone.

I asked her if she wanted me to put on any music in particular, but as soon as I did, she burst into tears.

I wasn't used to this.

Intense emotions were things I tried to steer well clear of because they never led to anything good.

"Tess... are you okay?" I asked. Her head dropped and the tears continued to spill. I went over to her and placed a hand on her shoulders. She immediately fell into me, as though she was melting. I tried to be as comforting as I could even though it didn't come naturally to me.

"Is this because of Hank?" I asked.

"I don't know what I'm going to do!" she eventually wailed, her beauty marred by the glistening tears and the twisted expression on her face.

"What happened? Did you have a fight?"

"I haven't even spoken about that to him yet," she cried. "But it's happened. It's happened and I'm not ready for it."

"What's happened?"

"A baby. I'm pregnant."

"Are... are you sure?" I asked. She stopped crying for a moment and glared at me. I guess a woman knows these things. She pulled her knees into her chest and panted deeply.

"Okay... so... wow. I mean, I don't really know what to say, congratulations I guess?"

"Oh yeah, congratulations. I have a baby with a guy whose parents don't want a black grandchild. That's just fantastic, right? And right in the middle of college as well. It was the worst time. And I don't get it because we're always careful. I'm always careful."

"I guess mistakes happen," I said, and smiled apologetically because it wasn't exactly helpful. "Well, look, I think the best thing to do is talk to Hank about this and then you know where he stands, and then you can figure out what to do. And whatever happens you have your folks and you have me and you have Linda and Bailey."

"Don't tell them. You can't tell them. Not yet," Tess said.

"Okay. Sure. Your secret is safe with me," I said.

Tess seemed relieved at this. "Do you want me to take you over to Hank's now?"

Tess shook her head, which surprised me. "I can't tell him tonight. Not before the game. It's not fair. He needs to be clear headed. He won't be able to play well if he has this going on."

"Tess, you can't keep this to yourself. It's too big for one person to handle."

"That's why I told you," she said pointedly. "I'm not telling Hank until after the game."

"Okay," I said, knowing that arguing with her wasn't going to do any good. "Can you still do the routine?"

Tess nodded. "I'll be fine. I just need to think, that's all, and hope, and pray..." she trailed away. Her life had changed dramatically in the blink of an eye and I hadn't truly realized how fragile it could be. She wasn't just a girl with her whole life ahead of her any longer, she was a mother to be, someone who had a whole other life to think about.

I did not envy her.

I also did not tell her that, for obvious reasons. I was about to make her a warm drink when there was a hammering at the door. The last thing I needed was some annoying neighbor. I was going to ignore it at first, but the hammering sounded again. Tess dragged herself up and let herself out the back, muttering that she needed to be alone. I was about to chase after her, but this damn person wouldn't stop hammering at my door. I eventually flung it open.

"What?!" I exclaimed, glaring at Bobby, who stood there swaying with a stupid look on his face. His eyes were bloodshot and even from here I could smell the alcohol on his breath. He carried a bottle with him as though he was some old fool who had drunk his life away.

"Aren't you happy to see me?" he asked, his words dancing around a hiccup.

"What are you doing here Bobby?" I groaned, rolling my eyes.

"That's no way to treat an old friend."

"We're not old friends."

"Then what are we?"

"A mistake," I said. Bobby didn't take kindly to that. He took a swig of his drink and glared at me.

"You don't get to talk to me that way," he said, pointing towards me. "You should have been lucky I ever bothered looking at you."

"Well, I don't feel it. Go and bother someone else Bobby. Better yet go home and tell your parents that you're gay. You'll thank yourself for it."

"I'm not gay!" he cried, and swung at me. The blow came unexpectedly, so I couldn't defend myself. He caught me right on the temple and pain blazed through my skull. I staggered back and I was unable to slam the door shut, so Bobby was able to take a lurching step into my home.

"Bobby, I don't know what you want here tonight, but you're not going to get it. It's best for you if you just leave."

"I can't leave Liam; don't you get it? I don't know what you did to me, what you planted in my mind, but I just can't stop thinking about it. I know you can't either. I still catch you looking at me every time we're in the locker room together. I know what you're thinking. I know what's in your perverted mind," his words slurred together and he lunged for me, trying to embrace me. I ducked out of his grip and bounded to the other side of the room, trying to use the couch to divide us. Bobby turned, still holding his bottle of drink.

"You're seeing things that aren't there, Bobby," I said.

"No!" he cried. "You poisoned me. You did this to me! And now I want you to fix it."

"I can't fix it Bobby because there's nothing that needs fixing."

"Just one more night. One more time. If I just feel you again Liam, that'll be enough. I just need to get it out of my system," he reached his hands out towards me, but I wasn't going to play this game.

"It'll never be out of your system Bobby. The best thing you can do right now is to go home and tell your parents that you're gay. There's no shame in it. The world isn't going to end."

Bobby laughed. It was a dry, cracking sound, as though the world was splitting in two. "It might not be the end of your world, but it is the end of mine. What do you think they're going to do? They'll take me away. They'll hide me away. I won't have anything anymore. It's not my fault. I never asked to be this way. I never wanted this. I never wanted you. It's all your fault. You did this to me."

"You can't blame me for all your problems Bobby," I said, but he wasn't listening to my words.

He swung again, but this time with the bottle. It hit the wall and smashed. Alcohol trickled out and now shards of glass were on the couch and the floor, while he held a shattered bottle. The jagged edge of glass stared at me.

"Bobby, just put the bottle down," I said, holding out my hands, trying to prevent panic from creeping into my voice. The last thing I needed was for the situation to escalate. "How about we call one of your friends? They can come pick you up and take you home and you can get a nice sleep. It's the game tomorrow. We should be well rested for that," I added.

"Just shut up!" Bobby screamed. His throat was raw and the sound of his shriek was chilling. I held up my hands, unsure what to do or say. He had been pushed to his limits and I did not want to test him further. I could see the hatred in his eyes. Whatever he felt for himself he had turned onto me, making me the focal point of his ire. I was glad that the girls had left, although part of me did want to see how Bailey reacted to Bobby being like this. Maybe this would be enough to stop her infatuation.

He snarled and looked like a wild animal. I kept a close eye on him and when he lunged, I was able to use my agility to dodge out of the way. I grabbed his arm and wrenched it, which made him drop the bottle. He was a strong guy, but thankfully the alcohol had made him sluggish. He struck out at me again, but I leaned back and watched his elbow fly past my face. I shot back with one of my own, jabbing my fist into his ribs before giving him a right hook that sent him flying. He groaned and staggered towards the door. Enough was enough. My hand ached. My head still throbbed. Bobby cursed at me and then left, slamming the door behind him.

I sank to the floor when it was all over, looking at the broken glass that had been shattered all over my apartment. I clasped my hand in front of my head and breathed deeply. That was too close. I don't know what had possessed him to come to my place, but I was going to have to take some measures to stop him. It was not going to be fun seeing him the next day. I just hoped that he would be able to focus on the game and that he would stop trying to blame me for everything that went wrong in his life.

Chapter Five

Finn

The world had changed. Everyone was looking at me. I could feel it. My heart pounded as I walked into practice and everyone turned to face me. I caught Matt's face. He looked away. I knew he had said something. There was a whisper that passed around the locker room and I knew it was about me. My heart sank. I had barely been able to sleep after I left Matt's because of what had happened. I kept trying to think of some way to explain it away, like saying it was a joke or something, but nothing made sense. There was no other explanation other than that I was gay, and now everyone on the team knew it. I felt so stupid because I had protected the secret for so long, only to let it slip at this crucial moment, and I had no idea what was going to happen next.

My hands trembled and my throat was dry. There was a lump lodged inside that wouldn't go away no matter how much I swallowed. A part of me wanted to speak to Matt, while another part of me just wanted to be swallowed up by the ground and disappear for all eternity. I kept thinking of Liam and how he would probably laugh it away. I bet this kind of thing happened to him all the time. Damn him. If I hadn't have seen him being so flamboyant and expressive, I would never have gotten the idea to take a risk. I should have just buried it deep down inside of me where it could be hidden, where I would never have to worry about it again.

The Coach called me into his office before I could speak to anyone about it. Nausea clung to my stomach and bile was slick in the back of my throat. I went to his office, which adjoined the locker room.

*

Coach stood up when I entered and gestured for me to take a seat. He closed the door behind me. The office was dotted with trophies and pennants and newspaper articles declaring his great achievements. Some of them ran back decades. I felt small sitting in front of him, this man who had experienced so much, who had control of the team and my destiny.

"So, Finn, there's been a few whispers this morning about something that you've been keeping from everyone," Coach said.

My head dropped and I gazed into my laps. My hands were clasped and I fiddled with my fingers. I nodded in response to his question.

Coach sighed. "I'm not going to lie to you Finn, I'm not that good at these kinds of things. I'm no guidance counselor. I'm the coach of the football team, and that's the way I'm going to handle this situation. I know this must be a difficult time for you and obviously you've been struggling with this kind of thing. I don't know what your story is or how many other people know, but the team knows, and as uncomfortable as it is for you, we have to address this in the right way. You're a good player and a valuable part of the team, but you should know that a team can only work if every player trusts each other.

Look I don't bear any ill will against you, but the fact is we have a big game coming up and I can't have this ruining our chances."

I couldn't believe what I was hearing. Ruining our chances? This is my life he's talking about!

"Is this because I'm gay?" I asked in a harsh, brittle voice. It sounded strange to utter those words out loud after I had tried to keep the secret under wraps for so long. It had all unraveled with one stupid mistake, one missed signal, one desperate plea for attention. Coach regarded me with a look of complete strangeness.

"No, it's not because you're gay. I couldn't give a damn what you do with your time. My job is to win football matches, but I can't do that with people who keep secrets from their team mates. I'm sorry Finn, but I really have no choice in this. I'm going to have to bench you for the game."

I leaped out of my seat. "No!" I gasped.

"It's the way it has to be. I'm sure you can figure all this out in time, but not in time for the game. Besides, I would have thought that you'd have plenty of things on your mind right now."

"I want to play Coach! I've been training for this. I've been practicing for this. I know I'm ready. I'm ready to break the streak."

"I'm sorry son, but it's not good for morale. The rest of the team hasn't had a chance to come to terms with the news yet. They're going to resent you. If you're on that pitch the whole dynamic is going to be messed up because they're going to be thinking of things other than the game, and I can't have that. You know how important this game is to the entire college, hell, to the entire half of this damned town. I can't let anything jeopardize it. I know this isn't fair and I know you're going to hate me for the rest of your life because of this, but I have to put the team first. You'll play again. You know that. You're just going to have to miss this game."

He spoke as though it was no big deal, but this was the game. It was the game where I was going to stake my claim on the world and etch my name into the legend of this college, and he was taking that away from me. They were all taking it away from me. Anger boiled within me and I began to tremble. I wanted to wreck his entire office. I wanted to wreck the whole school! There was no sense in it though. What would be the point? It wouldn't get me my place on the team back. I ended up walking out of his office, my shoulders slumped. The world seemed different as I left, crueler somehow, and my thoughts turned to Liam. He didn't have this problem. Everyone knew he was gay and they all celebrated him. I bet the football team hadn't tried to get him chucked out. I bet he could come onto whoever he wanted without fear that it would ruin his reputation. God, I bet he had even kissed a whole load of guys.

Suddenly a memory flashed through my mind, as though it had been unlocked by recent events. It was a memory that had niggled at the back of my mind, although I had always tried to push it away because I wanted to pretend that it hadn't meant anything. It was a memory of when we were young. Liam and I had been playing in the dining room of my house, sitting in a nook behind the door so that we were hidden. We were rolling toy cars around on the floor. He turned to me and asked me if I wanted to do something that adults did together. My skin burned. I knew exactly what he meant. My parents weren't the most obvious about showing affection, but Liam's parents were never shy about kissing each other openly and I had seen plenty of things on TV. There was a part of me that was disgusted by the thought. The idea of pressing my lips to another's seemed strange, but so many people enjoyed it so there must have been something to it. I was afraid, but I nodded anyway. I closed my eyes and sat there as Liam leaned into me. His lips brushed against mine. We were just kids and we had no idea what it really meant, but I knew that I liked it.

It only lasted a moment because we heard my dad's footsteps coming down the stairs. I had always been so afraid that he had seen something, that he knew. Liam and I had never kissed again because he moved away soon after that. I had buried that kiss deep down into my soul in the hope of never thinking about it again because it didn't do anything except bring me pain, but it had always been there, a scar of nascent love.

*

I was sullen as I was eating dinner. Mom and Dad were chatting amiably. Dad was in a surprisingly good mood. I knew that was going to change soon.

"You know it's not polite to remain silent at the dinner table. I don't mind you spending entire evenings in your room Finn, but this is family time and I expect you to honor that," Dad said.

"Don't be too harsh on him. I'm sure he's just tired from all the training he's been doing," Mom said gently. She was always the one who tried to soften Dad's blows.

Dad didn't seem convinced. "Well, I suppose you have been working hard. What do you think our chances are? Are the team confident?"

"Sure," I said.

"Does the coach have a good plan in mind? You're going to have to be crafty and smart if you're going to beat them. I know the last guy relied on passion, but that's not enough."

"He's pretty smart. I'm sure he has a few tricks up his sleeve."

"Good," Dad leaned back in his chair and smiled. "I'm looking forward to this game. I can't wait to see you take to that field and hold your head up high and really make a difference to this town. You know son, when we're young we all think we can make a difference in the world. We all have grand ambitions to leave our mark and have our names sung through the ages. Few of us get to achieve that. Most of us have to settle for raising a family and creating a legacy through our children, but you're going to be different. When you win this match, it doesn't matter what else you do in life, you're always going to be a legend around here and I bet you'll get free drinks in any bar you want."

I dropped the fork, suddenly feeling sick. How was I going to tell him? "Dad I... I hate to tell you this, but I've been dropped."

"Dropped? What do you mean you've been dropped?"

"The Coach just told me today. He said that he's going in another direction for the game."

"Another direction?! What do you mean another direction? They don't stand a damn chance of winning without you. You've played in every game already? What is he thinking? I'm going to have words with him. My son is not going to miss out on the biggest game of his life because of the whims of some damn coach," Dad threw his napkin down and rose from his chair. Panic flooded my heart because I knew what he was going to do. He was going to pick up the phone and call coach and then I would be in an impossible situation.

"Dad, you can't call him. It wasn't a whim. He had his reasons," I said softly. It was just enough to break Dad out of his fury. His skin was still flushed though, and his nostrils were flared like a bull's. I was already dreading what was going to happen and this did not make it any easier. He tilted his head. It took him a moment to realize what I was saying.

"What did you do?" he asked. I wasn't about to answer him. My mind was spinning, trying to think of a way to avoid this conversation but it was inexorable. It was a boulder that had been careening down the mountain of my life since my birth, and now was the point of impact.

"Is it drugs? Is it drink? What the hell are you into that could have caused him to drop you, Finn?"

"I don't think-" Mom said, trying to bear the brunt of his words for me as she always had, but this time Dad wasn't having it.

"I think you should give me some time alone with my son," Dad said. Mom opened her mouth to protest, but she knew, like me, that there was no sense in trying to change Dad's mind once he was convinced of something. She gave me a sympathetic look and left the room. I was rooted to my chair. Dad leaned forward, looming over the table like the specter of death.

"You need to be honest with me right now Finn. If you've been dropped because of something unfair then I will champion your cause and I will march through that school and cause a world of trouble for them, but if you've done something to jeopardize this yourself then you're going to have to face the consequences. Either way, you need to be honest with me," he said in a low, dry voice.

My heart hammered inside my chest. How could I be honest with him when he had spent his life telling me that he only wanted me to be a certain way?

"I didn't do anything to mess up Dad, but Coach does have his reasons. And it's not going to make any difference if you speak to him or not."

"But that doesn't make any sense. If you haven't done anything wrong then how can he have a reason to drop you?"

"There was a falling out with the rest of the team, okay? It was a misunderstanding, but Coach doesn't think it's a good idea for me to be on the same field with them."

"Is he serious? The whole point of being a team is that you put these differences aside for the good of the game. I'm not having this. I thought the man knew what he was doing!"

I have to admit that it felt good to have my father as my champion for once. I almost wanted to let him go ahead, but I could imagine how the conversation was going to go and I had to do it myself. I had to be the one to tell him.

"He does Dad. It's not just a difference of opinion. It's because I'm different. It's because I lied to them," I admitted. It felt like there was a stone in my throat as I spoke. This was never how I imagined the conversation happening, but it was unavoidable now. Dad might as well know. Everyone at school did by now. It wouldn't be long before word reached back to him anyway.

"Lied to them? I never raised you to be a liar. What on earth do you have to lie to them about?" he asked.

I looked up at him with a desperate gaze, almost begging him to twinge. I wanted him to know innately so that I didn't have to say the words. I wanted him to have a realization, for it to dawn on him, but he was absolutely clueless.

"I'm gay Dad," I said weakly. They were three short, simple words, and yet they were powerful enough to destroy my entire world. Dad took a few moments to react. It was almost as though I was watching a film in slow motion. His face twitched in confusion. He shook his head a little, and then he had to steady himself on the table.

"I never... you can't be," he said.

"I am Dad. One of the players found out and it spread around and so they decided they couldn't trust me at the moment," I said, but this had stopped being about football.

"You're gay?" he asked, as though it was the most shocking news he had ever heard.

"Is it really that surprising Dad? I thought you might have picked up on something over the years," I said.

For a moment I thought he might actually accept it. For a moment I thought things were going to be better than I had imagined, that this might end up being one of those inspiring stories I had seen on the Internet. It turned out that this was just the calm before the storm. His face changed and he looked away from me. He gasped, as though he had been punched in the gut.

"I'm going to give you a chance now to change what you just said. We can pretend that this didn't happen. Your mother doesn't have to know. We can just keep things as normal," he said in a low voice.

Now it was my turn to get angry. "This is normal for me Dad! This is who I am! I know I'm not the son that you wanted, but I'm the son you have. Isn't that good enough for you? I've tried so hard every damned day of my life to make you happy, but it's never good enough. Being me isn't good enough, is it? I can't change this, Dad. I didn't choose this. This is just me."

"It's not you. This isn't the man I raised," Dad said. Tears welled in my eyes. They burned and stung because my worst fears had been realized. I had no idea what to say to him then. I stared at him, this man who had always given me rules and discipline and structure, who had taken me to ball games and sat down with me to give me advice, this man who had spent endless hours after work standing in the yard to throw a ball with me. And now, apparently, that meant nothing. I staggered upstairs and threw myself on the bed, burying my head in the pillow. My sobs were suffocated, and all I could think about was how Liam didn't have this problem.

Chapter Six

Liam

Game day was a disaster. My lip was cut and swollen, and there was a big shiner right under my eye. Bobby wasn't much better. Tess was a mess, as she had a right to be I supposed. The girls all gathered around me when they saw the state of me and cooed, all except Bailey. She stood there, simmering in her anger for a while. Linda seemed distracted too, although she wouldn't say why. Tess asked me what had happened. I told her that I'd gone to the store and spoke back at someone I shouldn't have.

"You're a liar," Bailey said. We all looked up at her. "I saw Bobby come out and he looks just as bad as you. Why were you fighting with him?"

Bailey was one of my best friends, but I knew that wasn't going to mean a damn when compared to Bobby. She liked me, but she adored him. I sighed for a moment, trying to think of a lie that would be convincing.

"You know how much I like him Liam!" Bailey exclaimed. "He's never going to want to go out with me if one of my friends attacks him. How could you do this to me?"

"Believe it or not Bailey, but you weren't exactly the first thing on my mind at that moment," I said.

Bailey pouted. Her innocent features could be shrewish when she really tried. "I don't care Liam. I want to know what this fight was about so I can smooth it over. I was just getting close to him; I could feel it. This game was going to be the moment when we got together. But if you've messed this up-" she said. I glanced at Tess. The pain was aching over my face.

"I haven't messed this up for you Bailey. I can't mess up something that doesn't exist," I snapped. Bailey looked as though she had been slapped. I was getting tired of tiptoeing around her though. I wasn't about to pretend that I was the aggressor here when Bobby was the one who had threatened me with a broken bottle.

"There's no need to be like this Liam," Tess said. "She doesn't mean anything by it."

"She never does," I said, and then I turned to look at Bailey. As I did, Linda pulled out her phone and walked away. "I've been trying to protect you Bailey, but if you're going to be like this then I don't see why I should any longer. You're supposed to be my friend, but you're not giving me the benefit of the doubt. But maybe I've not been a good friend either. Maybe I should have told you the truth. You have to understand that this thing between you and Bobby... it's never going to happen."

"Don't say that!" Bailey cried. In the background I heard Linda let out a cry of her own, and then a sob.

"Liam," Tess said in a warning tone, but blood was raging through my mind. I wasn't about to let go of this now.

"Bailey, Bobby is never going to fall in love with you because he can't. He's gay," I said.

"No, he's not!" Bailey shook her head vehemently. "How would you even know that?"

It was the wrong question to ask. I tilted my head and gave her a knowing look. Horror spread across her face and her mouth formed a large oval. She shook her head as she paled.

"It was a party. We got drunk. He started coming onto me and I figured why not? But he's too afraid of people finding out. So, it's been a secret this whole time, although apparently he hasn't been able to forget about me because he came back for more last night. I said no, and he didn't like that answer," I rubbed my chin awkwardly. Bailey's lips trembled and then she screamed. Tess called after her, but she was already gone.

"You didn't have to do that. You just broke her heart," Tess said. I knew what she meant. It could have been done in a nicer way, and maybe at a better time, but she had been deluding herself for long enough and it wasn't getting any better. I was about to say that to Tess when Linda screamed and threw her phone to the ground, smashing it completely. She was shaking and held her hands to her face.

"He's fucking staying with her. She found out about us and he groveled to her to take him back. He always told me that he was going to leave her for me. He told me... he told me so many fucking things and he never had any intention of keeping his promises. He's a fucking coward," she said, and stormed away. Tess gave me a weary glance. She had her own troubles to think about, but even so she left in pursuit of Bailey and Linda, while I was left to nurse my wounds.

*

The stadium was like an inferno. I could almost smell blood in the air. The rafters were packed with passionate fans and additional police had been assigned to the game in case there was any trouble between the rivals. I hadn't really been able to concentrate on the preparations for the game. Bailey still wasn't speaking to me. Somehow, she thought it was my fault that Bobby was gay and that I was trying to steal him from her, despite me not having any interest in interacting with him whatsoever. Linda was moody and sullen, barely speaking, while I could tell that Tess was worried.

It wasn't the ideal preparation for our cheers. We had a reputation for being the most inventive and precise cheerleading squad in the region and we usually got cheers, even from the opposing fans. Not tonight. As soon as our music started playing the boos rang out. It might not have been enough to put us off our game if we had been focused, but we all had other things on our minds, and we were fractured. The thing about a routine like ours is that when one moment of timing is off it sends the whole thing into disarray, and it's almost impossible to recover from. Tess was being hesitant and careful in her moves, while Bailey was trying her hardest to ignore me. Linda just wasn't concentrating at all. It was a mess, and what made it worse was that the boos turned into jeers as the crowd realized we were failing.

It was a sign of the night to come.

The coach glowered at us because we had managed to give the other team a small victory before the game had even started. We didn't get many chances to cheer again through the night. It was a rout. You could clearly see that our team had spent too much time partying the night before. They had been arrogant and thought the game had already been won before they had stepped onto the field. The other team were vicious and ferocious, like wild animals swarming over the field, starved and hungry. Out of curiosity, I watched for Finn, but I didn't hear his name announced. It was only later that I spotted him on the bench. I wondered what had happened, because it seemed as though he had been quite an important part of the team.

It was strange to see him now. Our lives had taken us in different directions, but we ended up in the same place. I wondered if he could see me as well, if he had any regret about never responding to my letters. Had he been angry that I had left? It was hardly my fault. I was just a kid. At least he would have this measure of revenge on me, I supposed.

I sulked as I sat with the other cheerleaders, wondering if our friendship was ever going to recover from this. The game couldn't end soon enough. When it did we received glares from the players, as though somehow we were responsible for their performance during the match. The girls went their separate ways too, which left me at a loss for what to do next. I got changed and showered, and before I left, I was accosted by Bobby and a few other players.

"What the hell was that out there?" he asked, the same anger was in his eyes that had been there the other night.

"I could ask you the same thing," I said. It took everything he had for him not to hit me. Maybe he was afraid that if he was too violent, I would spill his secret.

"You were supposed to cheer us and create a good atmosphere for us to play in, but you messed up. You threw the whole night off," he said.

"You can't blame us for your performance. Maybe if you guys had spent more time preparing and less time partying then you might have actually stood a chance. They were just better than you tonight. Get over it," I said, trying to shake them off and walk away.

Before Bobby or any of the others with him could say anything else, they were distracted. I heard a whistle and turned to see Bailey standing there in just her panties. Her long auburn hair cascaded over her milky skin, descending close to her pink nipples. She tilted her hips and faked an air of confidence.

"Bobby, tonight was a fucking disaster, but I'm not going to let it end that way. I've been in love with you since I was a kid, and now I'm just going to lay it all on the line; I'm right here, waiting for you to fuck me. So, what do you say Bobby?"

The men around us all cheered. They were all staring at Bailey though. I was the only one looking at Bobby, and I was probably the only one who understood the terror in his eyes. I had to give Bailey credit though. She was a canny operator. Here she was, presenting herself to Bobby in a way that no straight young guy could resist. If he turned her down now then there would be questions asked of him, and eventually his friends would find out the truth. He was more petrified of that than anything, so Bailey would get what she wanted; a night with Bobby. Maybe it didn't matter to her that he was gay. Maybe she thought that she could change him, or maybe she just figured that having him was the most important thing in the world, even if he would never want her in the same way.

"How could I resist," Bobby said. I heard the dread in his voice, but everyone else was too busy cheering him on. He walked towards Bailey and wrapped his jacket around her. She looked the happiest she had ever been and gave me a spiteful look before she turned away. I think she thought she was proving me wrong somehow, but I knew in the end she would be the only one who was left unhappy.

I took the opportunity to slip away, hoping to escape the stadium. I hadn't been on this side of the city for a while, but the roads were still mapped out in my mind. I was filled with nostalgia and decided to go to one of my favorite places as a kid to take some time to myself. Maybe I could figure out what was going to happen next.

Chapter Seven

Finn

The historic game day to which, at one point, it had seemed as though my entire life had been building towards, went by in a blur. In truth it had lost its luster the moment I learned that I would not be playing. Coach had put me on the bench, but unless there had been a freak barrage of injuries nothing was going to get me on that field. The rest of the guys were still giving me the cold shoulder, acting as though it had always been their right to know. None of them came up to ask me how I was coping with it all. It made me wonder if I had truly been a part of the team in the first place.

My dad wasn't in attendance either. He said there was no point if I wasn't playing, but I knew the real reason was that he didn't want to spend much time with me. He had been keeping his distance, almost as though I had to be quarantined. Mom was sympathetic. She kept saying that he would come around, but she never seemed to do much to help him come around.

At the game I noticed Liam from the beginning, and I became charged with intrigue and anger. He moved so gracefully and his physique was even more impressive in person than it had been on the scouting video, but there was something off tonight. Perhaps the occasion had gotten to him, although he had never struck me as the type to be put off by things like that. Then again, it had been years since we had spoken. A part of me was tempted to talk to him, but I wouldn't know what to say. Besides, he was the one who had left me. It was his obligation to talk to me if he wanted to.

The game went better than any of us could have expected. Secretly I wanted us to get thrashed at the beginning so Coach would have been forced to change things, and then I could have risen from the bench and won the game for us. Then everyone would have been forced to accept me as a champion, even dad. But that didn't happen. Our rivals were a heartbeat slower than us, and in football that was everything. As soon as we scored a few points we relaxed into the game and our confidence grew. There were no misplaced passes, no sloppy mistakes, and the longer the game went on the more we realized that we could actually do it. I'll never forget the reaction at the end. The crowd erupted in this passionate frenzy. You'd have thought it was the Superbowl or something, but I guess it was to this crowd. Grown men were crying, some of whom I recognized as players who had lost this game in the past. This one victory didn't only break the streak, but it also seemed to redeem all those players who had lost in the past. They flooded the pitch and hugged and kissed each other. I wore an ironic smirk. There were so many close-minded people who had an issue with gay men, yet in the state of euphoria they were happy to hug and kiss each other with wild abandon.

It should have been my moment too, but the fact that it had been stolen from me soured it. My name would not be one of those that were spoken about in hallowed tones. Nobody had cheered me on or watched me take to the field. I was little more than a shadow, a passive observer who didn't deserve any accolades at all. I started to wonder if I had any place on this team again. I had just missed out on the most important game of the season, so what was the point in playing anymore? I bowed my head and rubbed my temples. There would be parties going on long into the night, but I didn't want to be a part of them. I just wanted to be alone.

*

I could have gone back home, but I knew dad would be waiting there for me. It wasn't as though he would actually talk to me or anything, he would simply glower and then leave, but his presence was enough to put me off going home. Even though I had always been filled with a sense that I did not belong anywhere, I had still always felt welcome at home. Now that had been taken away from me too and I wasn't sure how that was going to change. I didn't think dad was suddenly going to change his mind, but where did that leave me? Was I supposed to be a stranger in my own home?

I decided to wander the streets of my city. I dug my hands into my pockets and kicked errant stones away, sending them skittering along the sidewalk. In the distance I could hear the cheers of celebration as people continued to mark the victory. It was humbling to see how a city could be unified like this, and at the same time it was dispiriting to think that I was not a part of it. I ended up walking towards a place that I had favored as a youth, a park that was not too far from my house. It was eerie at night. The moonlight spilled onto the slide and swings, and the hollow darkness of the playhouse seemed as though it should have been filled with ghouls. I stopped short when I saw someone else in the park, sitting on a swing. I didn't want to mingle with the usual kind of person who spent time in a park at night, but there was something familiar about him, and then it hit me; it was Liam.

Breath caught in my throat as I stood there and looked at this man who had once been my friend, and was now my enemy. He was my opposite too. He was out and proud, whereas I was merely ashamed. Deep down I knew it was unfair to resent him simply for living a life that I could not live, but I still had this feeling that if he had stayed in touch with me, I might have turned out differently. I had always imagined what I would say to him if I ever saw him again, but now that I actually had the opportunity I was lost for words.

The swing creaked gently as he moved back and forth. He turned his head, and then he saw me. He rose from the swing. I couldn't glean any information from the expression on his face. The silver light cast an ethereal glow on his face, making him seem unreal. His eye was bruised, his lip swollen, but that didn't make him any less handsome. In fact, it only increased his allure. I kept my lips pressed together though, unsure of what was going to happen. We were technically heated rivals and my team had just routed his team.

"Hey Finn, it's been a long time," he said. I wasn't sure what I had expected him to say, but I hadn't thought he would be so casual about it. I suppose it's what was natural for him though. He took everything in his stride and nothing was ever difficult for him.

"Liam... I wasn't sure you'd remember me," I replied.

He smirked. "My memory isn't that bad," he said. "It was a good game for you tonight."

"Yeah, my team anyway."

"I was surprised to see you on the bench."

"I was surprised to be there," I said.

Silence hung in the air between us. The conversation was stilted. A part of me wanted to release all of my anguish in one torrent of emotion, while another part of me wanted to walk away and leave him behind, just as he had left me all those years ago. I ended up doing neither. He looked around the park.

"You remember when we used to come here?" Liam asked. I nodded. "You always used to hate going too high on the swings."

"I hated the monkey bars too. I was never strong enough to swing myself across. You liked everything though."

"It was fun," he said, shrugging a little.

"It was," I agreed, smiling at the memory. I hadn't been back to this park for a while, but the memories were still striking. It was surprising how strong the memories we made in childhood were. I could still feel the exhilaration as Liam would push me on the swings, goading me to go higher and higher, while I begged him to stop, shaking my head and closing my eyes and gripping the swing tightly for fear that I would be flung off and go soaring through the sky, never to land again. It was the same kind of feeling I had when we kissed, and now that I was in his presence again the memory of that kiss became more vivid. I struggled to keep it pressed down inside me.

"So, how's life?" he asked.

"It's okay I guess," I replied. "You?"

"Same. I thought you would be riding high after tonight."

"It's not as though I had a part to play in it."

"Yeah, why is that?" he asked. I frowned a little. Being with Liam like this was strange. We had a lot of history together, the kind of history that led to a natural intimacy, but we had also been strangers for far longer than we had been friends. I was longing to speak to someone about this, someone who might understand, but Liam and I had lived such different lives I didn't think he would be the one to comprehend the magnitude of what had happened to me.

"I don't think you'd get it," I said.

"Try me," Liam replied. His eyes sparkled with easy charm. He seemed relaxed, as though he knew exactly who he was and what his place in the world was like. The envy within me grew. I remembered how lost I felt when I realized that he had gone. There hadn't even been a goodbye.

"I really don't think it's something you'd want to hear about. And I'm not sure it's something I want to talk about."

"Sometimes those are things you need to talk about the most though. What happened?" he asked, an earnest sense of interest coming through in his words.

"You wouldn't get it," I repeated.

"Why?" he laughed, "because I'm not from this side of the city now?" the cavalier way he dismissed my concerns rankled me. I don't know why it got under my skin so much, but the feeling crawled around like spiders beneath my flesh. Things were so easy for him he probably never had any trouble with being gay. I bet he never even had to come out, he was just himself and people assumed he was gay because he never gave them any reason to think otherwise.

"No, because things have been easy for you," I said in an accusing tone, my words burning hot through the chill of the night.

He looked confused. "What are you talking about?"

"I've seen you up on that stage, so flamboyant and free with who you are. Everyone loves you Liam. Nobody is ashamed of you. You don't have to worry about what people think. You just are who you are and that's good enough for the world, but it's not the same for the rest of us. We still have to live in the shadows. We still have to hide who we are, and when we're not hiding any longer, we end up being shunned."

"Finn, what the hell are you talking about?" Liam asked.

Was he really being this obtuse? Couldn't he see what was happening? My hands curled into fists and I raised my voice, the shrill words shattering the quiet ambience of the deserted park.

"I'm talking about the fact that you're gay! You're gay and everyone knows it and nobody has a problem with it, and it's always been so easy for you. Everything has been. Life has just been handed to you and you haven't had to worry about people ignoring you or shunning you. You haven't had to live with shame every day of your life. You haven't had to hold this secret inside you and feel it rotting away your inside, knowing that you're missing out on so many good experiences because you just can't afford to be yourself. I bet you've had boyfriends and lovers and you haven't had to hide your attraction to them. You haven't had to pretend that you're just too focused on your work for a relationship. You don't have to wait for your life to begin. You're just living it. Do you know how maddening that is!" I fumed, breathing hard after the words had shot out of me.

Liam stood there, stunned. "I hadn't realized that it was, no," he said.

"Well, it is," I replied, and I wasn't finished there. "And you know what else is maddening? The fact that you just left without saying goodbye. What the hell was that about? I thought we were friends?"

"I didn't have much choice in the matter. I was just a kid! I didn't choose to leave," Liam cried out. Now he was raising his voice as well. He threw his hands up in the air.

"No, but you could have said something. You knew where I lived. You could have written to me."

"I did," he said. His words blindsided me. "I did write and you were the one who never wrote back. I wrote to you when you were settled and I wrote to you on your birthday and I wrote to you at Christmas, and then I stopped writing because I knew it wouldn't make a difference. I don't know what's going on with you Finn, but my life hasn't been all that perfect. You think it's easy for any of us? Get real... you know what? I don't need this. I have too much on my plate already. I don't need your problems as well."

He stomped past me and walked away.

"Sure Liam, looks like history is repeating itself. Just walk away again," I yelled in a harsh voice, although deep inside I was filled with regret. I stared at him as he receded into the distance and thought about what he said. Was it true? Had he sent me those letters? If so, then what had happened to them? I shook my head and walked away shortly after that, suddenly tiring of returning to my childhood. It seemed as though there wasn't a single part of my life that was not going to bring me anguish.

Chapter Eight

Liam

I was back in my apartment after the short visit to the other side of the city, and I was still stewing about what Finn had said to me. What was it with guys like him and Bobby, did they just have it out for me or were they assholes to everyone? I don't know where he came off accusing me of leaving him behind when he was the one too stubborn to reply to my letters. I guess time had warped his memory. I wasn't going to let it bother me though, at least that's what I told myself. Still, I found it difficult to shake him from my mind. Seeing him again had been a shock to say the least. It was one thing to stare at him from afar as he sat on a bench, but another to be within a few feet of him. He had grown up to be damned gorgeous as well. He had thick hair that flowed down his head like a mane, cute dimples on his face, and piercing eyes. His body was powerful too, stockier than mine because he needed more bulk as a football player than I did as a gymnast. He was a little shorter than me, but then again, he always had been.

I wasn't sure what had given him this chip on his shoulder, or why he blamed me for it. Why did he even think I had it easy in life? Being gay always led to a whole host of problems in a straight world. I guess something must have happened with his team. The more I thought about what he said the easier it was to piece it together. I guess he had been in the closet and someone had found out. They didn't take too kindly to it, so he had been benched. It was unfortunate, but it wasn't the first time it had happened. It still didn't give him the right to speak like that to me though.

Tess came round for dinner. I said I would cook. I needed the company and she needed to not think about things for a while. She looked paler than usual. I didn't think she had been sleeping well. I served up dinner and she sighed.

"I guess we have to talk about what's going on, right?" I asked.

Tess nodded. "That was bad. The game. I don't know how we're going to recover from this," she said.

"We'll get there. It'll just take time. It's not the first time we've had a spat."

"This is more than a spat Liam. We're spiraling."

"How are the other two? I haven't had a chance to speak to them yet."

"Linda is going crazy, while Bailey is just… she's never going to forgive you Liam."

"I know. I saw her after the game. She took Bobby away. Do you know what happened?"

Tess nodded. "They spent the night together. She was pleased as punch the next day. Said that you were wrong and that he definitely wasn't gay."

"Well, she's either deluding herself or he managed to put on the performance of a lifetime, but it's not going to last."

"You shouldn't have told her the truth," Tess said.

"I was tired of her bitching about Bobby. She needed to learn. I just wish it had worked out differently," I said, thinking about Finn. If I was right then he had been outed as gay and shunned by his teammates. When the same thing almost happened to Bobby, he managed to slip away from it all and end up sleeping with a girl. The world was never just.

"She's going to have it in for you now. You know what Bailey is like. She can be intense when she wants to be."

"I know," I sighed. "And what about Linda?"

Tess shook her head. "She's gone off the deep end. She got drunk last night and smashed her car. She said she was going to go around to his house and beg him to take her back. I've never seen her like this. I have to babysit her, and that's without what I've got going on."

"Have you told Hank yet?" I asked.

Tess looked away. "I told him before the game," she confessed in a small voice. "I meant to hold onto the secret, but I just couldn't. Now he's angry at me because he's saying that I confused him and put him off."

"He's angry at you?" I asked, incensed that he could react so callously.

"I'm meeting him again tonight. I'm going to talk to him about it then."

"But has he given any indication to what he thinks?"

Tess shook her head. "He said he didn't have time to process it because of the game. I don't know what's going to happen Liam, and I'm scared."

I put my arm around her. "Hey, it's okay. You don't have to be scared. No matter what happens I'm always going to be around, and I'll keep you safe, right?"

Tess nodded, although I could tell that she wasn't entirely convinced. "But I'm going to have to give up cheerleading. Everyone is going to look at me and judge me."

"If anyone judges you then just send them round to me, okay? I'll sort them out. I'm not going to let anyone hurt you, including Hank. You just stick by me, alright? I've got your back, no matter what."

"You're such a good friend Liam. I'm sorry that this all had to happen so close to the game," she nestled her head against my chest and her breathing calmed.

"It was a pretty big mess."

"The entire school hates us now. They blame us for everything going wrong," Tess said.

"People can blame us for anything, it doesn't mean they're right. They're just too afraid to face their own shortcomings," I said, thinking about Finn. I decided to tell Tess about it to take her mind off things.

"And he was really that angry with you?" she asked, after I had told her the short story.

"I think he's angrier at the world more than anything. I wouldn't be surprised if he's angry at his dad too. That man never gave me the feeling of being nice," I said, shuddering as I thought about the sound of his footsteps coming down the stairs and his stern voice. I wasn't sure if he even knew any kind words.

"So, what are you going to do? Are you going to speak to him again?" Tess asked.

"I don't know that there's any point. Whatever friendship we had died in childhood. I think he's just one of those people that I used to know in life. We drifted apart. Seeing him again was just a huge coincidence."

"I don't know, I like to think these things have some meaning in life," Tess said. Tess was always the type to look for meaning in things. I thought it was just a way of trying to find some order in a chaotic world, so it had never appealed to me, but it had struck me as quite a big coincidence that not only had Finn and I been present at the same game, but that we had chosen to go to the park at the same time as well.

"I think in life sometimes there's unfinished business," Tess continued, "and we don't always have the opportunity to go back and fix it. I think it might be a good idea for you to get in touch with him again. If you were friends once then you might still be again. It sounds as though you had a pretty good time when you were younger," Tess said.

I nodded along. "We had our moments. To be honest I did always get the feeling that we were going to be lifelong friends, before we moved away."

"Well, there you go then, maybe it's time for you to take back what was once yours," Tess said. To be honest I was thinking that I might need some more friends. Bailey hated me, Linda was falling apart, and Tess had her own crap to deal with. What's more is that the school was going to turn on me because of our poor performance at the game, and Bobby would be able to come after me if he wanted. Now that he had Bailey as a beard he wouldn't be as afraid of me accusing him of being gay, because he had Bailey to defend him. When I looked at it like that, things seemed a lot bleaker than they had been previously. Besides, something had irked me about the way Finn had spoken to me. I wanted to set the record straight. I wasn't content to be the enemy in his story when he was the enemy in mine. He'd had his chance to rant. Now it was mine.

*

I drove across the city divide; the long bridge that everyone took to be the point by which the city was halved. I remember being driven along this bridge when I was a kid. My folks kept telling me that we were starting a brand new adventure, and they made it seem as though things on this side of the city were more beautiful and far grander than they ever had been on the other side. I had kept asking them if Finn was coming with us. Now I was heading back to the old neighborhood. My senses were enlivened at the sight of it. I breathed in the air of the sycamore trees and remembered how the leaves used to blow across the street in the autumn. I heard a trill of a bicycle bell in the distance, and it brought back sunny days where Finn and I would ride to our heart's content, without a care in the world. Even then I knew there had been something different inside me. I wonder if Finn felt the same way.

I pulled up away from his house. I snuck around the back, remembering how we used to play cops and robbers all around this place. There were so many hiding places and neither of us had ever been able to gain the advantage over the other. Finn's bedroom was at the back of the house. There was a sloping roof over a back porch, which was currently deserted. I smiled at the thought of his mom baking a pie. There was always some sweet treat she'd have for us. My mom was hopeless in the kitchen, so I was always happy to have dinner with Finn. The more I spent time here, the more the memories kept flooding back and it surprised me just how happy I had been there. I guess over time

I had become jaded and thought only of the bad things. Maybe it was a coping mechanism, a way for me to pretend that my current home was better than this place. I crouched low and ran up to the back window. Given the way that Finn had spoken about his father, I guessed that Finn still lived at home. His dad didn't seem the type to give Finn any freedom anyway.

I gathered a handful of small stones and flung them up the house. They rippled against the window, creating a cascading sound that was like rain. I waited a couple of moments and was ready to throw another handful, when the window opened. Finn's face protruded.

"Liam? What are you doing here?"

"I came to talk," I said in a hushed whisper, not wanting his father to hear. "Things ended too abruptly the other night."

"I don't have any more to say."

"Well, I do. I drove all this way from the other side of the city. Come on, the least you can do is come out for a coffee or something," I said. For a moment I thought that Finn was going to be as obstinate as his father, but then he rolled his eyes. I guess curiosity got the better of him. He swung one leg out of his window and grabbed a hold of a pipe, before placing his feet against a lower ledge. I winced, afraid that it was going to buckle under his weight, but he shimmied down and jumped the last couple of feet, landing with a thud. He glanced behind his back and we ran away like mischievous children. For a moment we were young again, and it was as though no time had passed at all.

Chapter Nine

Finn

I don't know what had possessed me to come with Liam, but the fact that he had shown up unannounced meant that he wanted to talk about something important. I felt a little guilty about the way things had ended the other night. The more I thought about it the more I couldn't understand why he would lie about sending letters, so if he was telling the truth then what had happened to them? There was something not quite right about this, and I wanted to figure out the truth.

I rushed away from the house, glancing back, afraid that dad would see me. It wasn't as though I had been grounded or anything, but things were still tense between us. I was waiting for the moment when we would clear the air, but it hadn't happened yet. Maybe it never would. Liam had an old car that somehow looked stylish, despite the faded paintwork and the reluctant chug of the engine.

"Is this thing going to hold together?" I asked.

"She's got it where it counts," Liam said. He slapped the dashboard with his palm and the car jerked into life. Loud jazz music filled the vehicle. "I hope you like this. I can't change the station," he said, having to raise his voice to be heard over the music. One of the windows didn't work properly either, so was perpetually open a crack. The wind blew in. It wasn't much of a car, but still, it was more of a car than I owned. We drove into town and headed towards a bar. It was quiet at this time of day. I was a little worried that people might have looked at us with suspicion, but they minded their own business. I thought Liam would order a fancy cocktail, but instead he got a beer. I made it two. Nerves flickered within me as we took a seat near the window. I had no idea what was going to happen.

I wrapped my hands around the cool glass and watched the bubbles rise to the froth.

"So, what do you want to talk about?" I asked, trying to stop my voice from shaking with nerves. The swelling in Liam's lips and the bruised shine of his eye were fading.

"I guess I just wanted to clear the air a bit, you know? Running into you the other night was a, well, it was a shock to the system. I think we maybe have different ideas of what happened when I left. Maybe even over the years we've begun to resent each other. I thought it was better that we got to know each other properly, face to face, rather than let all this fester inside us."

"I suppose that's the mature way to handle things," I said, although I felt myself shuddering inside. I had never been so good at confrontation. I guess that was just another way in which Liam was different to me. He had always been the one to lead and I had always been the one to follow, but just because he was here it didn't change things.

"I'm glad you agree. So, listen, what's all this about not getting any of my letters? Did you really think I was going to leave without saying anything?" he asked.

"You did. I felt for sure you were going to send me something, but you never did."

"And I'm telling you that I did, Finn. Something must have happened to them along the way. I always thought you just wanted to forget me because you never replied. Eventually I knew there was no point in trying. You weren't ever going to get back to me."

I heard a twang of emotion in his voice. For the first time I actually believed that this meant as much to him as it did to me, and that he had been as hurt as I had been. All this time I thought I had had a monopoly on these emotions, but it seemed that that wasn't the case.

"I didn't know where your new address was. I couldn't have written to you. It's why I was waiting," I said forlornly. For a moment I was back to that boy who pressed his nose against the window, looking at the house nearby, wondering if Liam was ever going to return. At that age I had no idea how things worked and I just assumed that his family could have moved back if they wanted to. When I looked at him now, he was a fully grown man, but there were still elements of the boy I knew. There was still a sense of mischief in his eyes. My gaze fell to his lips and I started to think of the kiss we had shared. I was too shy to bring it up now.

"I didn't want to lose touch with you Finn. You were my best friend," Liam said. His words made my heart shudder. A smile twitched upon my lips. I couldn't quite believe how much I had needed to hear those words, but it was as though dawn spread across my soul and I felt lighter than air. I was about to tell him that he was mine too, when suddenly I noticed something in the window, or rather someone. It was dad, and he looked furious.

Moments later the door was forced open and he burst in.

"So, this is where you are! I should have known you were with someone like him," he said spitefully, his gaze narrowing and pointing straight at Liam. The air became thick with tension and a drumbeat pulsed behind my eyes. I knew if I wasn't careful this situation could escalate to the point where it exploded.

"It's Liam, dad, my old friend. We ran into each other the other night and thought we'd just catch up," I said, trying and failing to defuse the situation.

"I know very well who he is. I thought we had gotten rid of you a long time ago," dad said. His voice dripped with bitterness and hatred. I had never heard him speak this way about anyone before. It was as though I wasn't even there. He stared past me and straight at Liam. His body was rigid, his arms were clenched to his sides and his hands had rolled into tight balls. It looked as though he was going to explode. Liam narrowed his eyes.

"So, it was you then. I always thought it was. I kept asking my parents why we had to move away and they would never tell me. They just looked at each other, pretending that I was too young to understand. But deep down I knew it was you. I could feel the hatred burning inside you," Liam said, rising from the table slowly.

"Hatred? What hatred? Dad, what's going on?" I asked.

"Haven't you realized yet Finn? He's the one who stopped my letters from reaching you. He's the one who has stopped all of this. He drove me and my parents away. Why? Are you afraid of my sprinkling some of my gay fairy dust on you?" Liam asked, his tone mocking, his face filled with anger. I could barely believe it. Was dad really behind all this? I knew he hated the idea that I was gay, but would he have really gone so far as to drive Liam's family away?

"I don't give a damn what you do, I just don't need you doing it in my face, or around my son. You've already had too much of an effect on him already. I knew you were going to confuse him. I kept being told that I was overreacting, that this didn't mean anything, and then I come down and I see you two..." he couldn't even get out the word. He scrunched his face up and looked as though he was about to be sick.

"Kissing," Liam finished off for him. I was stunned. I had always thought that we had been able to hide that from dad. I guess I must have gotten it mixed up in my mind. I sat there, utterly horrified. All of this was because dad was afraid of me being gay. Maybe everything had. All those nights when we had been playing ball together... was that just so that I would have a 'straight' hobby?

Now it was my turn to feel sick.

"Shut your damn mouth and leave my son alone. We don't need you here. We don't want you here. I got rid of you a long time ago and I don't want history to repeat itself," dad said.

Liam shook his head. "Oh no, you don't get to do this old man. You're just a bully, and I was done with bullies a hell of a long time ago. I'm not a kid anymore. You can't scare me. You can't intimidate my parents. If you want me to go somewhere then you're going to have to make me."

"Gladly," dad said, rolling up his sleeves. I couldn't believe what I was seeing. I opened my mouth in an effort to try and say something, but no words came out. I was so stunned. Liam walked out from the booth and stood toe to toe with dad. Now, dad was a strong guy and had been athletic in his youth, but his youth was a long time ago. His muscles were not as taut as they had once been, whereas Liam was in the prime of his life. What's more, he was raging with anger. Dad snarled. I was about to leap up and get in the middle of them when dad went to clip Liam around the ear, but Liam reacted quickly, more quickly than dad expected. What was it with the older generation underestimating youth? Liam blocked the blow and then hit back with one of his own. He cracked dad on the jaw and then slammed his fist into dad's stomach, sending him to the floor. Dad slumped down like a sack of potatoes. He clutched the side of the table to help him rise to his feet, but his hand slipped away. His breaths were heavy and the bartender had come rushing out to tend to the fight.

Liam stood over him, his face filled with fury. He was panting too, and he looked like a wild animal. I was caught between them both. Dad glared at Liam, and he looked at me expectantly. I knew he wanted me to stay with him, to go back home, to be chewed out and have another damn lecture about hanging out with the wrong people. I'm sure I was going to be grounded again, like I was some kind of errant teen. I was supposed to be an adult. I was supposed to be able to make my own choices, but he was never going to let me do that.

I ended up stepping around him and leaving the bar with Liam. We ran to the car and he revved the engine. We sped through the streets and returned to his apartment. My heart was hammering in my chest. I couldn't actually believe what had just happened. My mind was reeling and I wasn't sure what to think, all I knew is that Liam had just stood up in defense of me. Maybe he wasn't the real enemy after all.

Chapter Ten

Liam

I hadn't meant to let things get so out of hand. My knuckles stung and pain continued to reverberate through my arms as I drove through the city. I glanced in the rear-view mirror to make sure that he wasn't following me. I wouldn't have put it past him. I looked across at Finn, who was pale. He wasn't saying anything. I thought maybe it was better that he didn't. I had just clocked his dad and sent him falling to the floor. It was never a good thing when you realized your parents were weak.

I had been burdened with the same knowledge for years, although it hadn't been clear to me until this very moment.

His dad was behind it all. He was the source of all this misery.

I drove him back to my apartment and grabbed him a soda from the fridge. He sat on the couch, still with that numb and dumb look on his face. At the park I thought he had a lot of his father in him. That temper, that rage, it was the kind of thing that should have been siphoned out of the gene pool, but right now I just pitied him.

"I can't believe it. I can't believe he would do something like that," Finn said.

"Are you sure about that? Because I can sure believe it," I replied. I was still standing. The adrenaline flowed through my body, making it impossible to stay still or sit down. I paced around the apartment and leaned against the fridge.

"He was so angry," Finn said.

"That's what people get like. That's what people are still like now. You think we've made progress. You think the world is a more tolerant place, but then you come across someone like him. Sometimes I think it would be better if we still had to keep ourselves hidden. When we're out like this it makes us easy targets for people like him."

"And you punched him," Finn said. I guessed he was going through everything in his mind again, trying to make sense of it. He spoke softly. I felt a little guilty, not for hitting a bully, but for the fact that the bully was his dad.

"I'm sorry. I didn't mean it to go that way, but he just really got under my skin," I said. Finn shook his head in a vague manner and then frowned.

"Were you right? Did he really do this? Did he keep us apart?" Finn asked.

I stopped pacing and put my hands on my hips. "Look, all I know is that day after we... had that moment, your dad came round my house that night. I didn't hear what was said, but afterwards mom and dad looked at me strangely. They were speaking in whispers and that was the first time they started speaking about moving. I don't know what your dad said to them, but he can be a pretty intimidating guy. When I said that I wanted to write you letters mom acted as though it was a bad idea. I wasn't sure why at first, but now I guess I know. She must have been relieved when I got no reply."

"I always thought you had forgotten about me. I thought that you had stopped caring," Finn said. He lifted his gaze and our eyes met. So many years had passed. We had been boys, but now we were men. Even so it was impossible to forget the memories we had created together, to forget the friendship that had been present between us.

"I could never forget about you Finn. You were my first kiss," I said. The words lingered in the air between us. He had grown into a good looking guy. I wasn't sure what he wanted out of this though, and I wasn't going to press the issue. We both had a lot on our minds.

"You've been my only kiss," he said.

"Wait, you've never..." I asked.

He looked at me and flashed an embarrassed smile, shaking his head. It was starting to make sense now. "I guess it's pretty hard to do that kind of thing with a dad like him," I said.

Finn sighed. "Yeah, it is. I had to keep it quiet for a long time. I buried it inside myself. But then recently, I don't know... I was getting signals from this guy on the team and so I made a move. Took me all the courage I had. Turns out I was wrong. He told everyone else on the team, I got dropped because I was told they couldn't trust me for keeping a secret from them, and then when I told my dad I wasn't playing in the game I had to tell him why because he was about to raise hell for me."

"I can imagine how that conversation went," I muttered.

"Exactly. He wasn't happy at all. Somehow, I think he believes I've betrayed him. I don't get how the logic works in his mind," Finn says.

"That's the thing; there never is any logic. They're just scared. They're all scared of us, as though we're some kind of monsters."

"I don't want to be a monster. I just want to be close to someone," Finn said. I could hear the weight of emotion in his voice. It was no wonder he had seen me as the enemy before this.

"You must have been so lonely," I said.

Finn nodded. "You were the only friend I've ever been close with. Football has been the only thing I've been good at, but I knew I could never be myself because of the jokes the guys made in the locker room. I know what kind of things they would have said, and I knew they would have felt self conscious about being in there with me after they knew. And then there was dad... I always hoped deep down that if I ever told him he would be able to put this weird hatred aside and just support me, that he would just be able to treat me like a son for once in his life. I guess he never wanted me to be my own person though. He only ever wanted me to be the man he wants me to be."

"Some people are like that. I got lucky with my folks. I think they knew from a young age what I was going to be like, and they never made me feel different for it."

"You were lucky," Finn said. I couldn't help but notice the tension in his voice. He kept his gaze away from me, as though if he was to look at me again then he would end up erupting with anger. I wanted to show him that he wasn't entirely correct.

"Sure, I was lucky in a lot of ways, but it's not been as easy as you think. I know you see me up there dancing around and being all flamboyant, but that's not the way things have always been, and it's not easy to get a steady boyfriend either. I still have to deal with prejudice every damn day of my life, and there are nights when I have to cry myself to sleep because I don't understand why the world has to be so damned hard for people like us." Finn looked pensive as I spoke. He didn't seem inclined to say anything else, so I continued speaking.

"Let me tell you a story. When I was in high school I wanted to be on the football team too, but unlike you I wasn't going to hide who I was. Everyone knew that I was different. At home I was allowed to be this way, so I figured there was no harm in being this way at high school either. But the football team was different. People kept telling me that I was going to throw like a girl, or that I couldn't handle it. In tryouts I proved them wrong, but that still wasn't good enough. When we got back in the locker room all of them pointed to the shower, telling me that I had to go in there myself because they weren't going to have me perving over them. Then when I was inside, they all threw their soap at me. They laughed at me and insulted me and they made sure that I was never going to feel welcome there. They bullied me away and sure, I could have probably fought it, but I didn't have the energy.

So, I became a cheerleader instead. And I try and make the most of it, but it's not what I always wanted to be. Every time I'm up there doing another cheer, I keep thinking about how I should be running out on the field and making a play. I just pretend like it doesn't bother me because if you're a part of the joke then sometimes it doesn't seem so bad, but I've been up and down the country doing this and people aren't kind anywhere you go. I have a few friends I can trust, but it definitely hasn't been easy. Why do you think I wanted to get jacked in the first place? I had to learn to defend myself."

"I'm sorry you had to go through that," Finn said after a pause. His words were heavy. I sighed and sank on the couch beside him. I leaned forward and ran my hand through my hair.

"It sucks for all of us Finn. It always has and it probably always will."

"It makes you wonder what the point in any of it is, doesn't it?" Finn asked. I could hear the sense of despondency in his voice. It was a question I had asked myself many times over. He was at a point in his journey where he wasn't necessarily ready to accept things as they were. He was still so young in that respect, having kept things a secret for this long.

"There is no point, is there? We all just have to try and take what little happiness we can when we can. It's why when we find someone who actually understands us... well... we have to try and make it count, don't we?" I asked. There was a moment of silence that passed between us. I knew things were still tense between us. I didn't know how far or how close he wanted to take things. We had been through a lot together and had shared so much, but did any of that really matter when we had spent a lifetime apart? I decided to test the waters.

"I'm sorry that guy betrayed you. I know how hard it can be to put yourself out there."

"It doesn't seem like it, considering you get to at least be with other people," Finn said, remembering earlier when I had referenced having secret and brief flings with men.

"You know it's not all that great, right? I have to listen to my friends having deep and loving relationships when all I get is a fumble with someone who is too ashamed to accept who they are. I might have had experience Finn, but I haven't had a relationship. I don't know what it's like to go out into the world and celebrate with someone. But I do know what it's like to put yourself out there, to feel the fear that comes with the excitement. I had to do the same thing many years ago, when we were just boys."

Finn looked up at me. "You mean when we..." he said, trailing off. I nodded. "There are times when it feels like a dream. Sometimes it's felt as though it never happened at all."

"It happened," I reassured him. "It was my first kiss. Our first kiss. I know it never amounted to anything more, but that still makes it special."

"I thought you just did it to try something out. I thought we were playing."

"I guess I didn't realize the significance of it, but I wasn't playing. There was always something between us Finn, at least until your dad got in the way."

"I can't believe he would do such a thing," he said, leaning forward and placing his head in his hands. I was beginning to regret mentioning his father. I wasn't sure what was going to happen between us, but I could feel there was something there, something that lingered from childhood. There was a bond between us that gave rise to intense feelings and maybe that was why we had held such resentment for each other. It was all a misunderstanding though. I couldn't help but think about what my life could have been like if we had stayed in touch with each other, if we had been there to support each other and help each other through the minefield of high school. There were so many moments that had been robbed from us and I was beginning to think it was time for us to take some of them back.

"I know," I said, placing my hand on his back. "But that's just the kind of man your father is, I'm afraid. I wish it wasn't the case."

"I don't know how I'm going to go back there. I don't know what I'm supposed to say to him. How can I live in the same house as him after I've learned that he's been treating me like this?" Finn asked.

"I don't know, but if you need a place to stay you can always crash here."

"I can?" he asked, looking around at me. There was a lock of hair that drooped down his forehead. It was alluring. His face was fresh, his eyes bright, and his lips looked smooth. My heart was inflamed by the sight of this man that I had known since I was a boy, and all the feelings of enmity between us just slipped away.

"Of course you can," I said, chuckling to myself. "I know things haven't exactly gone to plan in our lives, but I'm not about to turn you away. I know how hard things can be. I know how lonely things can be. Sometimes all you need is for someone to reach out and remind you that you're not alone," I said, lowering my voice to a whisper. My hand ran down his back and along his arm, feeling the swell of the bicep. Desire surged within me as I felt his broad shoulders. My fingers ran along the bristling hairs of his forearm. I felt a lump in my throat. I knew what it was like in his position, how the fear and the excitement could mix together and become so overwhelming that it made you want to run away. I hoped that he would not flee though. I hoped it with everything I had.

He turned slightly to face me. He did not make any attempt to take my hand away from him. He just had this mystified look on his face, as though he couldn't quite believe that this was happening.

"We gave each other our first kiss Finn, but now let me give you your first proper kiss," I whispered, reaching up to cradle his head. I pulled him into me. I knew he was never going to make the first move. He had been scarred by his bad experience. I closed the distance between us and felt us blurring together. His breath was warm and sweet. I closed my eyes and pressed my lips against his. A hot, strong bolt of energy lanced through me and I felt as though I was on fire. He pulled his head away, gazing at me. His lips moved, but he uttered no sound. I smirked and then kissed him again. I went slow, moving my lips deeply. I thrust my tongue into his mouth, playing with his, tasting the warm depths of him. The more we kissed the more he got used to the sensations, and the more he relaxed. I ran my hand along his neck and down his chest. I felt the tautness of his muscles, and then it dropped deeper. His moans were sharp and low, grunting like an animal. I could feel the tension rippling around his body and I knew it would be bulging within him. I wanted to see how much he had really changed. My hand slipped down his stomach and ventured farther, eager to touch him, but he shivered and he gasped and then he uttered a word I did not want to hear.

"Wait..."

Chapter Eleven

Finn

I felt like a fool for pulling away. I know I should have just given myself over to the sensations and enjoyed everything that I had ever wanted, but the nerves bubbled inside me and I could not control them.

"Wait," I said, and pulled back. I could sense the disappointment and dismay within Liam.

"What's wrong?" he asked.

"It's just that I'm... I'm not used to this. I don't know... these feelings... they're all very overwhelming."

Liam grinned. "They're meant to be," he said. He might well have argued against everything being easy for him, but there were certainly some things that came far more naturally to him than they did to me.

I nodded. "I get that, it's just that this is all so new."

"And I get that," Liam said, "but at some point you're going to have to take the plunge, it might as well be with the guy who you had your first kiss with," he said, and then he laughed. "Look, I'm not going to pressure you into anything because I know what a big deal this can be. Frankly I wish I had waited a little longer too, but it's not going to get easier the longer you wait. Sometimes you just have to throw yourself in at the deep end. Have you never even been naked with anyone else before?"

I shook my head, wishing that he hadn't asked me because I hated admitting this stuff. Liam rose from the couch and I was afraid he was going to ask me to leave. I didn't want that to happen, I just wanted to feel at ease.

"So, I guess you've only ever been intimate with yourself. It's a whole different ball game when another person is involved. I'm happy to take it slow with you Finn, but I still want to keep moving," as he said this he pulled his shirt over his head and tossed it aside, displaying his taut muscles. My gaze roved over his body. His skin was smooth and tense, with a slight tan. There was a cluster of freckles near his hip. He caught me looking and I guess he thought I was looking at something else down there. He grinned and peeled away his pants. I wondered how it could be so easy for him to flaunt himself like this. I wished I had his confidence and his poise. Even now I could feel myself tensing up, but that didn't stop me from looking.

He pulled his pants down and was standing in athletic underwear, tight things that wrapped around his waist and clutched everything together, although at this moment it looked as though things were going to explode. There was a fine line of hair that ran down from his navel towards a widening shadow of hair, which became visible as he peeled his underwear away. I felt as though I should have told him to stop, but the words never made it beyond my throat. His underwear fell down his legs and he kicked them away. He turned, showing me his taut ass and his long back. I could barely believe he was standing in front of me. I was still too nervous to touch. He took my trembling hand and lifted it to his body. The moment my fingertips touched his skin I felt as though I was being scorched. His skin was so smooth. Heat radiated from him. He dragged my fingertips along his skin, but my gaze was focused on his erection. He must have been turned on by performing this whole show for me. He was long and thick. The tip stared at me and I was filled with an innate need to touch it and kiss it. It felt as though it was everything I ever wanted and more, and he was standing right in front of me, offering it to me. How could I possibly turn it down? How could I possibly be a coward and run from him?

"Would you like to touch it?" he asked, noticing how I was staring at it rather than him. I nodded. He took my hand along his waist. I felt the hair on his skin, and I could feel the air shimmering with heat. A lump formed in my throat as my hands brushed against the hardness. I blinked and my breathing deepened. He let go of my hand then, seemingly trusting me to feel my own way. I caressed his shaft, bringing my fingers all the way around the circumference. I felt my way along the rivers of veins that wrapped around him and gave this thing life. He shivered when I felt his tip. I then wrapped my fingers around him and held him tightly, stroking back and forth, just as I did when I was by myself. I had seen other things on the Internet, things that I wanted to try. I wasn't brave enough to do that yet though. I just wanted to feel him.

He murmured his delight and arched his neck back.

"That feels so good," he said, and a wide smiled adorned his face. His lean and sculpted body was standing in front of me, towering in all its glory, and my hands were touching him, touching another man! Suddenly it wasn't as scary as I thought it was going to be. My hands and wrists moved slowly, massaging him. "If you want to try using your mouth you can," he said.

I licked my lips and then swallowed my nerves. I hoped that I was good enough for him. I leaned forward. When I inhaled, all of my senses were stimulated by his scent. It was as though I was being filled with him. He stepped forward. My hand ran down to the base of his shaft and then I reached up with my mouth. I closed my eyes as I touched him with my lips. My tongue flicked out. I enjoyed the taste of him, and whatever happened next came naturally to me. I opened my mouth wider and took him deeper, sliding my head up and down his erection just as I had with my hands. I again went slow, coating him in my saliva, whirling my tongue around. He seemed to like this. His hand cradled my head, his fingers ran through my hair. The air was filled with his terse moans that grew deeper and deeper. I followed the tone of them because they guided me into knowing what he liked. I opened my eyes as I took him as far back as I could, feeling his warmth scorching the inside of my mouth. I gasped and he smiled and cried out "Yes, YES!"

I sucked him hard and tasted all of him. I fell into the rhythm of pleasuring him and in that moment I didn't want to do anything else. It felt as though I was made for this.

"Do you want to know what it feels like to make a man come?" he asked. I could barely hear him over the cacophony that was sizzling within my mind, but I did want that. I wanted it very much. He widened his stance and braced himself, tensing his muscles. His skin was flushed with arousal and I knew what was coming, but I had no idea how it was going to feel. All I knew is that I was going to suck him dry. I felt the tremors in his body and I heard the rising, raging moans, and then I felt him in my mouth. There was a shudder, a quake, and then this pulsing sensation as this warm, cloying liquid swam over my tongue and trickled down my mouth. It was hot and lustful and I kept my lips wrapped around him as he came, determined to keep every drop.

None of it left my mouth.

Liam let out a deep, satisfied laugh as he opened his eyes wide and seemed to be seeing the world for a new time. He stretched out his arms and made another satisfied moan, and I felt so good for being able to make him feel like that.

"I can't believe you just took all of my cum. You know that wasn't required, right?"

I shrugged, the taste of him continuing to linger in my mouth. "I guess it just felt right."

"Fuck yeah, it felt right. It felt amazing. God, that must be the best blow job I've ever had," he leaned down and wrapped his hand around the back of my head, taking a firm grip of me. He pulled me into him and kissed me deeply, his tongue sliding as far back into my mouth as it could go. He licked his lips afterwards. He must have enjoyed tasting himself in my mouth.

"I can't help but notice that you're still dressed. Are you still wanting to take things slow? Because it feels as though things are ramping up," he said, "and I want to see what you're hiding." He fell to his knees and placed his hands on my thighs. A smile twitched on my lips. I guess it was only fair to show him what I had going on.

I nodded a little as I rose. We stood in front of each other as I pulled off my top. He helped me. It felt so strange to be doing this with him, although at the same time it was incredibly natural as well. It was almost as though this was the way things had always been meant to be, and we were just following the natural course of the world.

As soon as my top was off, he was biting his lower lip and grinning with delight. He ran his hands all over my broad chest and biceps, digging his fingers into my taut muscles. He kissed my neck and I tingled all over, as though pixies were dancing upon my skin. I could already feel myself getting hard. He grazed his hand along the outline and I almost doubled over, such was the intensity of the moment.

"I'm not going to last long if you touch me," I whispered, feeling embarrassed.

"I'll take that as a compliment," he said, and just like that all my doubts vanished. He kissed me deeply again as he pressed his body right up against mine. Sweat prickled and heat rose in the air, and it felt as though nothing was going to be able to pry us apart. I gasped and grunted as he fumbled with my belt. I was in too much of a daze to do anything.

"There we are," he said, as he pulled them down and wrestled them away from my ankles. He took me in his hand. I wasn't as big as him, but he didn't seem to mind that. A powerful surge of energy crashed all the way through my body and I felt as though I was going to explode within moments. Pleasure swam inside me and it felt as though my body was alive for the first time. A light was shining on me where before I had been standing in the shadows. He nudged me lightly and I fell back onto the couch, grateful to not have to rely on my legs to support me any longer because I could feel the strength slipping away from me. All the blood was rushing to one particular part of me and I knew it wasn't going to stay there for long. I had wanted this for such a long time. The excitement was a throbbing crescendo and all he had to do was stroke me and I was driven out of my mind. My chest rose and fell sharply, while my heart was a hammer in my chest.

"I'm going to..." I gasped, before he took his hand away. A whimper drifted out of my mouth and I looked at him through my hazy vision, wondering what kind of cruel torture was this. Was this all some kind of trick to get back at me? Were we still enemies?

He placed his hands on my thighs and looked up at me, grinning again. "Before you come I've got a little trick to show you. Believe me, it's going to change your life," he said. "Just tilt your head back and close your eyes, and if anything feels strange then it's meant to feel that way. Just let it happen," he said. His voice was intoxicating. I was already under his spell, so he might well have been able to say anything to me and I would have done it. My head lolled back and my breathing deepened. His hands continued to rest against my thighs and I wondered what he was going to do. At first I thought he was going to suck me as I had sucked him, but he didn't seem to want to get me off just yet.

Then his hands began to move. They slid up my thighs and back to my cock, or so I thought, but at the last second they took a detour. One of them rubbed me while the other one was taken away for a moment. When it returned I could feel the wetness dripping from it. Liam murmured as he nudged my legs open. I was self conscious, but I was too dazed with desire to resist him. As he said, I just let it happen.

And I was glad I did.

What followed was the kind of radiant pleasure I only believed existed in movies and stories. It started in the molten core of my body and then crashed through me in a rippling wave. It felt as though there was something alive within me, and I couldn't believe I had gone my entire life without feeling pleasure like this before. He stroked me and toyed with me. His fingers were like magic wands, conjuring wild sensations that careened through my body. I was so sensitive, having never been touched by anyone like this before. I twitched and spasmed and cried out loudly, but whenever I opened my eyes to see Liam in my blurred vision, he was smiling. I think he liked my inexperience. I guess it was a way for him to relive his first forays in his sexual awakening.

My hands fell limp by my side and I let these waves of pleasure ebb and flow within me. Liam was a master and knew how to wield his hands expertly. He curled them and twisted them at just the right time, finding all the sweet spots that were hidden within me. My throat ran dry and I gripped the couch, trying to brace myself against all the twisting sensations that were writhing inside like wildfire. It was strange to feel this great even though my cock wasn't being touched at all, and it was the first time I ever considered that I might have other erogenous zones. There was so much I had to learn, and if Liam was game for it then he would be the perfect teacher.

My eyes shot open as his fingers did something wild. I don't know how to describe it because I couldn't see. I can only say that it felt as though I had just been given an electric jolt. My cock throbbed and Liam chuckled. All these noises and sensations were pulled together in a storm of dancing lights that flooded my vision. I tried to speak, but the words were getting choked in my throat. I could feel it all coming out of me, waiting to flood me. I tried to wait longer. I wanted it to last longer. I never wanted this moment to end, but my body was weak and it needed to release this lustful pleasure that had built up inside it.

When I came, I came hard. It erupted out of me, hot and thick, streaming over my thighs and stomach. I even felt some of the drops hitting my chest. I groaned as I came, unable to stop it, and I heard Liam clapping.

"There we go. There he is," he said.

"I'm sorry," I gasped, my head rolling to the side.

"What the hell do you have to be sorry for?" he asked.

"I just... I wanted it to last longer."

Liam smiled. "It's not like this is going to be the only time," he said. There it was. That was exactly what I needed to hear. I wasn't sure how it was going to work or what the particular details were going to be, but all of that was inconsequential. Just knowing that he wanted to see me again, that this wasn't some kind of one off miracle was all I needed to soothe my soul. I breathed out my relief and sank into the couch, still covered in the fluids of my desire.

"Come on, let's go and get you cleaned up, otherwise it's going to dry and you're going to be all sticky," he said playfully. Somehow I didn't think he would mind me being all sticky. He led me to the shower and turned on the showerhead. A jet of water streamed out and steam soon filled the room. He held my hand as I stepped in, and then he got in after me. He handed me a bar of soap and it wasn't long before a lather formed in my hand. I handed it back to him and we began washing each other. I was in a daze as I watched the soapy bubbles trickling down his body, along his gorgeous muscles. I was convinced I was going to wake up within moments, and that this was a mere fantasy.

But it wasn't. He was flesh and blood, close to me. I pressed my body against him again. We kissed as the water surged around our mouths and cleansed us of sweat and stickiness. I traced lines down his body and breathed in the clean scent of the soap. I rested my hand against his waist and smiled as we broke apart from a breathless kiss. When the shower was over we dried each other off and then we put on some underwear, heading back to the couch. He grabbed a soda and some chips from the fridge and then came to sit beside me. I couldn't think of it being any more perfect. I realized as I was sitting there that this was all I had ever wanted. It was all I had ever needed. I tried to not let my heart get carried away, but it was difficult to rein it in. I was with the man who had given me my first kiss, and now that same man had given me my first proper orgasm. I couldn't help but wonder what other new territory we were going to explore together, and I knew it was going to be a hell of an adventure doing so.

Chapter Twelve

Liam

"What a day it has been," I said, as I sauntered back to the couch, handing a soda to Finn. I ripped open a bag of chips and stuffed a handful into my mouth. Fooling around always made me hungry. I took a moment to enjoy the sight that was currently sitting on my couch. Finn was a glory to behold. His years of athletic training had honed his body into something that resembled the prime of man. There was a light bed of hair that ran down the middle of his body. It was fun to touch. The rest of him had been fun too. I loved the way it had all been so new to him. It reminded me of how I had been when I first started exploring my sexuality. I had been so sensitive too... although I hadn't been blessed with such a patient teacher.

"It has indeed," he said, and the dazed, almost high expression finally left his face. I wondered if he had been brought down to earth and was thinking about his dad again. I was filled with a little bit of regret. I mean, I didn't have a problem with standing up to bullies and giving them a thump if necessary, but it was Finn's dad, and it would only make things more complicated for him. "I've really enjoyed this though. It's been something that I've wanted for such a long time Liam. I don't think you actually understand how painful it's been," he said.

I gave him a sad smile. "I understand," I said, and took his hand, squeezing it gently.

"I can't believe I spent so many years hating you," he said.

"I know, but life is funny that way I guess. It makes you wonder what our lives would have been like if my folks hadn't moved away. We would have still been friends. Maybe we would have turned out to be something more as we got older."

"I think we would have, although it's not as though we could have gone to prom together or anything."

"What did you do for prom?" I asked, curious about whether his and mine experiences had been different.

"I went with Maggie," Finn said, and seemed a little embarrassed.

"Oh, sheesh, how was that?" I asked. Maggie had always been a strange girl.

"It was fine up until the end. I mean, you know what's supposed to happen at prom. Anyway, I was ready to drop her off for the night and she told me that she wasn't ready for the night to end. She kissed me even though I tried to stop her, and if I hadn't known I was gay then I would have figured it out. She wouldn't take no for an answer so I told her that I'd be right in, I just needed to fix something in the car. I guess she thought I was being coy and needed to find a condom or something. Anyway, I just drove away and went back home. I saw her again a few months later at the mall. She still looked angry," Finn said, and then let out a small chuckle. "What about you?"

"I never actually went to prom. I knew that I wasn't going to get anything out of the night, so I just didn't bother going. I sat alone and I drank and I hoped that college was going to be better than high school."

"Has it been?"

"For the most part, I guess, but in other ways there are times when I feel like I'm still waiting for my real life to begin. I know that seems stupid, I mean, it doesn't get more real than this, does it?"

"No, I guess it doesn't. But I don't think it's stupid. There's always a sense of wonder. I mean, I still feel like I'm a kid sometimes. I still live with my parents, and I've never been able to express myself, and with a dad like mine I've always felt as though I've been held back."

I nodded slowly. "What are you going to do about your dad?" I asked.

Finn sighed and took a handful of chips, idly tossing them into his mouth one after another. I watched his tongue flick out and collect the crumbs that lingered on his lips. It was such an innocuous thing, and yet I found it incredibly sexy.

"I have no idea yet. Part of me just wants to run away, but I know that isn't going to do any good. I can't just ignore this. I can't just let him keep thinking this way about me. It's so old fashioned. I don't have some disease that is ruining my life. This is who I am. I need him to see that."

"He might not be ready to see it though," I said.

"I know." Finn arched his head back and let out a long sigh.

"You're welcome to stay and crash here for however long you need," I said.

"I appreciate that, but the longer I stay away the more this is going to fester. I need to speak to him. I need to sort this out, otherwise I'm never going to have a relationship with them, and I'll never be able to have a relationship with anyone else either. It's always going to be this issue that needs resolving."

"Then I guess you had better go and speak to him," I said.

"Will you be waiting when I get back? If he doesn't kill me," Finn said. I know he was joking, but there was a hint of doubt in his eyes.

"Of course I will, Finn. I've waited this long after all, I might as well wait a little longer," I said. Finn squeezed my hand and leaned into me to kiss me again. This time it was a softer kiss, more reminiscent of the first one we had shared. Other men I had been with had been rough and cruel and demanding. None of them had been innocent. It's what set Finn apart, and I guess it's what made me like him more than all the others. I watched him get dressed with great disappointment and then I wished him luck, hoping that his dad wasn't going to go nuclear on him.

*

A little while after Finn left there was a hammering at the door. I had pulled on some clothes and cleaned up the place a little, so at least I didn't have anything to be ashamed about. I opened the door to find Tess standing there.

"Where the hell have you been?" she glared. Her eyes were filled with fury and I knew instantly that something was wrong.

"I've been taking care of some things. What's happened? Is it Hank?"

"Oh, Hank is a whole other story, it's Linda."

"What has she done?"

"Well we know who she was having an affair with. It was Mr. Simmonds."

"Simmonds?" I had to take a moment to search through my memory and find the name. "The guidance counselor?" I said. We had all assumed it would be some professor, if it was anyone at the college.

Tess nodded. She folded her arms and paced around the room. "She smashed the windows of his car and painted all these words like 'liar' and things. She printed out all these pictures of them together and stuck them on his windscreen, and then she stripped to her bra and panties and sat there. She kept saying she was waiting for him to come by. She's lost it Liam, she's absolutely lost it."

"Oh God, well where is she now?"

"The cops have her. I just went to see her and she's in a bad way. I can't believe we ever let it get this far. We just treated it like a joke."

"It's not our fault. It's Simmonds' if anything."

"Yeah. You better bet I'm going to be on at the college for this. It must have started when she went to see him for depression, do you remember?"

I nodded. "I never thought he would be such a creep."

"No, neither did I. So I've been running around trying to deal with that, and you and Bailey have both been AWOL."

"I'm sorry," Liam said.

"It's fine," Tess dismissed, waving her hand in the air. She seemed to have gotten over the first flush of anger. "Everything has fallen apart anyway. Bailey is in a world of her own now. You should see her posts on social media. She's even started a new video channel where she catalogues her adventures with Bobby. It makes me sick. We all know she's living a lie, but it's just become this ultimate fantasy to her and she won't answer any of my calls or texts. I guess she knows I'm going to tell her the truth, and that's the last thing she wants to hear right now. How did it all go so wrong Liam?" she asked, and she seemed overwhelmed. She went to sit on the couch, but I guided her into a chair.

"You... might not want to sit there," I said. Tess looked confused for a moment and then rolled her eyes.

"You had a guy over here. Great. So while I've been running around trying to take care of everything you've been getting laid. It's nice to know that some things don't change," she said in a sharp tone.

"It's not like that Tess. It's not a guy, it's the guy, the one I was telling you about," I began, and then proceeded to tell her all that had happened between myself and Finn. She softened upon hearing this and even smiled.

"I guess it's good that at least one positive thing is happening in this crazy world," she said.

"What are you talking about? There's your baby as well. A new life is always something to be celebrated," I said. I didn't necessarily believe it, but it seemed as though it was the right thing to say in this situation. Tess had a despondent look on her face though. She sighed and her shoulders sank. She ran a hand through her hair. I noticed now the bags under her eyes and the strained look in, well, just about everywhere.

"Tess, what's going on?" I asked gently. I reached out and touched her knee. That was enough to set her off. Tears cascaded down her cheeks and she collapsed into my arms. She shuddered and shook and it seemed as though all the strength had left her. I held her as tightly as I could, trying to be as comforting as I could, but it took a while for her to be able to tell me what was wrong.

"He doesn't want me. He doesn't want us," she sobbed, her words getting lost in the forest of her sorrow.

"Hank?" I asked, although I don't think I really needed to make it a question.

Tess nodded.

"You spoke to him?" I asked.

She nodded again and dried her eyes. She sniffed back her tears in a deep breath, but it didn't stop them from coming. "I kept calling and calling and eventually I went to his place to see him face to face. He told me that he was sorry and that he was trying to figure things out. I told him that didn't mean he got to shut me out. Anyway, that stuff didn't matter. He kept me outside. I should have known something was wrong then. He told me that he had spoken with his parents about it and they thought that it just wasn't the right time for a baby. He said that he was still so young and had so many years ahead of him, and he didn't need to make that kind of a life choice right now. I knew he was just parroting their words though. I told him to be a man and tell me how he really felt. I wanted to hear what he wanted. He told me he loved me. I asked him if that was going to be enough. He looked back to that big mansion of theirs and he shook his head. He told me then that he was afraid of what was going to happen. He didn't know how to live without their support, and they weren't going to give it if he stayed with me. I told him that I was scared as well. Didn't he care about that? He said that he did, and he said that if I ever needed any money then he would find a way to make it happen." She let out a dry, humorless laugh. "I can't believe he actually thought money was going to solve the problem. I guess he is a lot like his parents after all," she said.

Anger welled inside me. If there was one thing I couldn't stand in life it was bullies. I had already stood up to one of them that day and I wasn't going to waste the opportunity to face another.

"This isn't right Tess. He's being a jackass and he needs to know it. He can't just get away with this. He can't knock you up and then act like he's the victim in all this."

"But what can I do? I just have to try and move on."

"There's always something we can do. Look, you stay here and take care of yourself. Just switch off from the world for a while," I said, moving away from her. Tess grabbed my hand.

"Don't do anything stupid Liam. Please, it's not going to change anything. It's just going to make a whole lot of trouble for yourself."

I shrugged and flashed a cocky grin. "I've been getting into trouble my whole life Tess. I'm not about to stop now. And I'm not going to let my best friend get treated like this. It seems like it's just you and me now. We have to take care of each other, and if Hank isn't going to stand by you then it's up to me."

I left before she could stop me or try and talk me out of it again. The cocky grin vanished from my face as soon as I left my apartment. I knew where Hank was going to be, and it was time that someone talked some sense into him.

*

The football team was practicing on the field together. I saw Bailey in the stands. She glared at me as I passed, but she didn't say anything. I didn't have time for her anyway. If she wanted to throw her life away on empty love then so be it. The team were laughing and tossing a ball around as though they didn't have a care in the world. I strode past Bobby and noticed how tense he got. Maybe he thought I had come here for him.

Maybe another time.

As soon as I saw Hank I made a beeline for him. I pushed him down to the ground. He wasn't wearing his helmet, but he was wearing some padding.

"What the hell kind of coward are you? You think you can knock a girl up and then just walk away because your parents tell you too? I thought you were supposed to be a good man. Tess thought the world of you. When you love someone you're supposed to do anything to protect them, even stand up to your parents. Get your ass out of your head and be a boyfriend, be a father, be a fucking man!" I cried, my words so vicious that spittle flew my lips.

Hank pushed himself to his feet and I had garnered the attention of everyone else.

"It's none of your business!" Hank cried.

"She's my best friend. Of course it's my business. It's more my business than it is your parent's."

"I'm going to make sure she's okay!"

"Oh yeah, you're going to throw money at her. That's what all rich people do when they want to make problems go away, isn't it? I bet you never even loved her in the first place. You're sick Hank. Maybe it's better that you do stay away. I wouldn't want you to poison your kid with this kind of behavior."

By now the rest of the team were gathering around us. I knew I was outnumbered, but I didn't particularly care.

"Just walk away Liam. It's nothing to do with you," Hank said again, but I wasn't done. However, I was interrupted by Bobby.

"There's no need to start making trouble around here Liam," he said.

"Oh fuck off Bobby. I am not in the mood for you right now," I snapped.

"I'm sure you're not in the mood for any of us. I've had word that you've been spending time with someone from the other side. I guess it wasn't a coincidence that the cheer was so bad when we played them. I should have known you were going to play for the other team, and now you owe us. You cost us big," he said.

I rolled my eyes. This was the last thing I needed. "What the hell are you talking about Bobby? The only people who cost you the match was yourselves, because you were more concerned about partying than actually training," I said. As I looked at him I noticed a flash of jealousy in his eyes. This wasn't about anything other than me seeing Finn.

"Then why the guy from the other side of the city? There's something going on there."

I don't know why he was goading me in front of everyone like this, but I was not in the mood to keep things a secret any longer. "Oh yeah, sure, I guess coming to my apartment drunk and wanting to fuck the night before the game was good preparation, wasn't it? That's right guys, Bobby loves cock," I exclaimed, but as soon as the words were out of my mouth Bobby was upon me, slamming his fist into the side of my face. I was groggy and staggered back. I barely had enough time to raise my fists to try and block the second blow before he struck again, this time the blow was powerful enough to send my head snapping to the side. I tried to fight back with a limp strike, but it only hit the padding.

"You don't get to come here and accuse us with these lies! Stay out of our way!" Bobby cried, and hurled more insults and more accusations at me. I guess it was easy to make me the bad guy again. A circle of guys formed around me. At any other time of my life this might have been a dream come true, but they only had one thing in mind. By insulting one of them I had insulted all of them. I was the outsider and they were about to make me pay. Fists pummeled into my face and chest. Air was driven from my lungs. I was pinballed between them all until I eventually fell to the ground. I curled into a protective shell, although it didn't do me any good. My mouth filled with the metallic taste of blood and I groaned in pain as the darkness set in. Tears stung my eyes and I just wondered why... why did it have to be this way?

Stars danced in front of my eyes, but in the distance I could hear a high pitched voice. It was Bailey. She was begging them to stop, telling them that I'd had enough. I guess she hadn't lost all her heart after all.

"Get the hell away from here. This doesn't concern you," Bobby said sharply.

"Bobby!" she cried. I heard another loud slap, and then I lost consciousness.

Chapter Thirteen

Finn

I had gotten a bus back home. I now stood in front of the only home I had ever known. It was supposed to be a place of safety, a place of refuge. At this moment it filled me with dread. I wasn't sure what I was supposed to do or say, or even if I was wanted here. I clenched my jaw and walked up to the door. I thought about knocking, but then decided just to open it. I poked my head into the lounge and the study, eventually finding dad sitting on the back porch, gazing out at the yard.

"Took guts to come home," he said, without turning to face me.

"Where's mom?" I asked.

"She went out," he said. My heart sank a little. It was a potential ally that was absent, although given mom's track record in standing up to dad I didn't think it made that much of a difference.

"Dad... about what happened earlier..."

"He's a menace. That's exactly why I don't want you hanging around with people like that. He confused you when you were younger and now he's back to make things more complicated. All you need to do is focus on school and football and everything will be fine," dad said, cutting me off, but he was doing that thing parents sometimes did where they spoke at you rather than to you.

"Dad, stop. Stop being so afraid. Liam didn't confuse me. This isn't anything anyone did to me. It's just the way I am. I'm not crippled. I don't have a disease. I just love a different kind of person than you do, that's all. It's really nothing to be afraid of."

"I'm not afraid!" dad snapped, and this time he did look at me. I saw the shining bruise on his face that had been left by Liam. I cringed with embarrassment. Such a thing should not have happened to him. There was a time when I believed dad was immortal and invulnerable. Now I could see that he was just a bitter old man.

"Dad, you're so worried about me being gay that you haven't even taken the time to actually ask me how I feel about it. Don't you think over the years I would have loved to come to you and ask you questions about things? There are so many things I've been afraid of, and I haven't been able to turn to you because I was afraid you'd react this way. It's been so lonely. I tried to make you proud, but deep down I knew that you would always be disappointed in me when you found out the truth, and I knew you were going to find out eventually. I just... I just hoped that when the time came you might be able to react with a little more patience and understanding, that's all. I'm still your son. I'm still the same Finn that you played catch with. I'm not any different. I don't understand why it's so difficult for you to accept me."

"I do accept you!" he exclaimed. "It's the world that doesn't. I know how cruel the world can be, especially to people like you. When I saw you and Liam kissing I knew that you were on the wrong path. I just wanted things to go easy for you Finn. I wanted you to be able to enjoy life, to feel free, to get through it all without any scratches on you. I knew that I wouldn't be able to protect you from all the prejudice and the insults that were going to be thrown your way. I just wanted you to have a quiet life surrounded by people who love you, that's all. I just wanted you to be normal."

"I am normal Dad, at least normal for me. This is just who I am. It's who I want to be. I just want to be that person while being able to have a relationship with my father as well, but if you aren't able to do that then something big is going to happen between us. I can't change who I am, and I've spent enough time hiding. I'm not going to go back in the closet. I've been holding myself back for too long. I've been trying to be what everyone else wants me to be, and it's time for that to stop."

"Are you going to go out with that boy?" he spat the last word with derision. I sighed inwardly. After what happened it was always going to be difficult to sell him on the idea of me and Liam going out together.

"He was just standing up for me dad, and standing up for what he believes in. I think you'd actually respect him if you just got to know him."

"Look, I know this is your life and I'm going to try to not stand in your way. This may not be the life I wanted you to have, but it's the way you are, fine. I guess I'm going to have to adjust to that. But he hit me. He humiliated me. I'm not about to welcome him around this house again, and if you still choose to spend time with him then it's you who are making this situation difficult. If you want to be respected then you have to give respect, and Liam is not welcome here," he said, pointing a finger at me. Even when I stood up for myself there was still going to be a measure of control exerted upon me. I wasn't sure if dad truly meant this or if he was just trying to make himself appear strong again.

I was thinking about what to say when the phone rang. It was Liam.

"Hey!" I answered brightly, although suddenly I felt self conscious because I knew Dad wasn't going to like me speaking to him. However, it was a woman's voice on the other end of the line.

"Hey, is this Finn? This is Tess. I'm Liam's friend. Something... something has happened. He's in the hospital. I'm going to send you a picture. I think if you could come that would be great. I think he'd like it if you were here. I just... he's in a bad way. I'm sorry if this catches you off guard. I'll text you the details," she said.

"Okay," I said in a daze as she rang off. My phone buzzed almost immediately afterwards as a picture was sent through. I gasped and staggered back, almost dropping my phone in the process. His face was swollen and beaten. His lips were cut. I could barely see his eyes. He looked groggy and he was hooked up to wires. My heart trembled and it felt as though my insides folded in on themselves.

"What's going on?" Dad asked.

I showed him the picture. He snorted. "That asshole probably deserved it. Guess he pissed off the wrong guy," he said.

"Dad, shut the fuck up and take me to the hospital." He looked shocked that I had sworn at him so directly. He furrowed his brow and I could sense that another argument was coming. It was the last thing I wanted to do, but my emotions were running high. I had no idea if Liam was near life or death.

"I'm not-" Dad began. I knew exactly what he was going to say. He was going to say that he wasn't going to approve of my relationship with Liam and thus he wasn't going to take me to the hospital, but I wasn't going to give him a chance to say it.

"Dad," I said in a warning tone. "If you want to accept me and be my father then you need to accept that I'm going to spend time with people you don't like. I know you don't like Liam, but I do. I've liked him for a hell of a long time and because of you we've missed out on a lot of years together. I don't know what the hell you were thinking keeping those letters from me, but you owe me this. You owe me because you took away the best friend I ever had and you made me resent him. You made me hate him. You made him my enemy, but it didn't last. And now he's lying in a hospital bed and you're really going to try and stop me from going? If you don't take me yourself then I'm done. I'm going to walk away from here and you're never going to see me again, because I guess you'll be happier that way," I said, glaring at him. For a moment I thought he was going to tell me to keep walking, but I think he knew it was not an empty threat. Reluctantly he grabbed his car keys and led me to the car.

*

The journey was tense. He followed me into the hospital. I met a tearful Tess. There was another girl near her who was staring into space. I think I recognized her as one of the other cheerleaders. I had no idea where the third one was though. Tess gave me a hug and then quickly told me what had happened, how Liam had been defending himself. She looked towards Bailey and told me that she had been there and she had tried to stop it. Bailey looked up at me, and when she did so her auburn hair fell away, revealing a sharp mark where someone had hit her. It seemed as though they had done a real number on Liam.

"Do you hear that Dad? He's the kind of man who stands up to bullies. Yeah, he's a real asshole," I said, as I walked into the room. I hated seeing Liam like this. His eyes were slits and his breathing was haggard.

"Still want to date me?" Liam asked. He laughed, but it ended up being a cough. I guess laughing wasn't a good idea. He told me that he had some broken bones and internal bleeding. I held his hand and tried to hold back tears. He struggled to speak, so I didn't try and have a conversation with him. I just sat with him and let him know that I was there. I told him that I had spoken with dad and nothing was going to stop me dating Liam. I told him that when he was fully recovered we were going to have a hell of a time together.

I hoped it wasn't going to be an empty promise.

Chapter Fourteen

Liam

I felt drowsy and heady because of the painkillers. They did their job, although it made it difficult to focus on my thoughts. Finn was there and I was glad for his company. He was on the verge of tears, and I think secretly he was a little glad when he left so that he could cry. I guess he didn't want to do that in front of me. Maybe he figured that I had dealt with enough already. The next person through the door wasn't who I expected though. It was Finn's dad.

He loomed large in the doorway. I wondered if he was going to put his hands to my throat and finish what the football team had started. He looked rigid with tension and seemed to struggle to get his words out.

"My son thinks highly of you," he began. "I've just been speaking to your friend. She says that you got in this mess because you were defending her against a guy who wanted to toss her to the sidewalk." I said nothing in reply. He continued, "I never wanted my son to be gay, and not because I'm a bigot, which I know you probably think I am, but just because I wanted life to be easy. But I guess I got things mixed up somewhere along the way. A good life can't be an easy life. If you're going to stand up for the things that matter then you're going to get bruised, and I guess I'd always like my son to be the kind of man who puts his body on the line for the sake of his friends. I know I can't take back the past, and if I'm being honest I'm still not sure that you're the best choice for Finn, but you are his choice. I don't want to lose a relationship with my son over this, so I'm not going to stand in your way. I just wanted you to hear it from me so there's no misunderstandings. You've been through a hell of a lot. I just don't want Finn to go through the same thing. If you can protect him from that then we're not going to have a problem," he said. He turned and walked out of the room. It felt as though I had been visited by a ghost. I had that same kind of chill crawling down my spine.

If that wasn't enough Bailey came into the room. She looked sheepish. She hung her head to the side to ensure that her hair came across her face like a veil, but I could see the bruise on her skin. I clenched my fist in anger. How could he have done this to her?

"I'm sorry Liam. I tried to stop them," she said, her words trembling with sorrow. "I've been such a fool. I really thought he loved me." She placed her head in her hands and wept. I didn't appreciate how she had treated the rest of us, but I wasn't about to punish her for this. It seemed as though she was doing a good job of that already. Besides, Bobby had probably done a number on her as well.

"You just wanted it to happen so badly that you tried to force it to happen. I don't blame you. You just wanted your fantasy to become real."

"I thought he was different. I couldn't believe it when he started beating you. I tried to get him to stop and then he... he..."

"I know," I said gently. "Bailey, I'm just glad that you're seeing him for who he truly is. You deserve someone better than that. You deserve a friend better than me as well. I shouldn't have gotten with Bobby, not when I knew how you felt about him. I should have told you the truth sooner as well."

"I wouldn't have believed you," she said, flashing a toothy smile. She wiped her eyes and seemed a little more relaxed now. "I want things to go back to normal."

"Me too. Tess is going to need all of us," I said.

Bailey glanced over her shoulder. "That guy is pretty cute. I'm looking forward to getting to know him better."

"Sure, just don't fall in love with him. He's mine," I said, smirking at her. I yawned then and leaned back into the pillow. I could tell that the painkillers were beginning to wear off because it was starting to crawl through my body. I was beginning to feel drowsy as well. They stayed with me for a little while, including Finn, but then I slept. I had a feeling I was going to do a lot of sleeping.

*

It took about a month before I was fully ready to return home. Tess, Bailey, and Finn were all regular visitors at the hospital. Linda unfortunately was tied up in legal matters for the time being. It was going to take a lot to help her out. I was glad of the company because life in the hospital was a drag, and the pain took a while to go away as well. However, the bruises faded and I was back to having my winning smile and handsome good looks. Tess gave me and Finn a ride back to my apartment when I was discharged. She asked if I wanted anything, but I think she knew Finn and I needed some time together. He led me to the bedroom and I sank down, glad to feel the comfort of my own bed again.

"So, will you tell me next time you run off half-cocked to take on an entire football team?" Finn asked crossing his arms.

"Hey, I think I would have stood a chance if they hadn't been wearing their padding. They're all just cheats at the end of the day," I said. Finn shook his head and laughed as he drew the curtains, casting us in darkness. It had been a strange courtship, where all of our dates had taken place in the hospital bed, or occasionally on a short walk around the hospital grounds. We hadn't been able to do anything like the sort of thing we had done the last time we were here.

"When I'm fully recovered we'll have a good night out. We'll get dinner somewhere, maybe catch a movie too, make a real night of it," I said.

Finn nestled beside me. "I don't mind if we just stay right here. My favorite place in the world is with you," he said.

Sometimes his sweetness was cloying. "You're not like any other guy I've known," I said.

"That's probably why you like me so much," he replied, and kissed me. I giggled and relaxed into the kiss. I winced a little too.

"Are you okay?" he asked, a look of worry coming over his face.

"I'm fine. It's fine. It's just going to take me a while to get used to moving again," I said.

"Well you just sit back and relax. You're at home now and you deserve to let all the strain and the tension wash away," he said, planting kisses at the base of my neck, running over my Adam's apple. I murmured with delight as his hands ran over my body. The window was open and a light breeze drifted through the curtains, but otherwise everything was still and quiet. It felt good to lose ourselves in our own little world. His hands roamed all over my body and his lips followed suit, leaving a trail of kisses along my shoulders and chest, before descending down my stomach. I watched him and felt his breath drifting along my skin like a wave of fire. A ball of pleasure swelled within me and felt as though it was going to burst. Fuck, it had been a long month.

I let my arms fall beside me as he ravished me. His tongue flicked out and it wasn't long before he was down near my groin. He bent over me and held me in his hands. Touching me the way he did had already made me hard. He ran his hand up and down my shaft, running his thumb over the smooth tip. I shuddered as nerves were fired off. Then he kissed the rivers of veins that rippled around me, his tongue stretching out to coat me in his saliva. I looked down and saw myself glisten. I listened to the way he sucked me. It was a feast for the senses and I just felt myself being lost in this miasma of pleasure. The air crackled with heat and as I closed my eyes I felt myself soaring higher and higher through the air, as though my soul was breaking free of my body and ascending to a different plane, while at the same moment these sensations were so deep within me, so primal and animalistic that they were stitched within the tapestry of my very being.

His breath tormented me. My heart quaked. I watched him take me into his mouth, but this time I didn't want him to taste me. Not yet. I wasn't ready.

"I've been practicing a few things," he said, as he flashed his gaze towards me, making me feel so naughty and dirty and fortunate at the same time. My eyes rolled into the back of my head as he did this thing with his hand and tongue that I couldn't fathom, all I knew is that it sent me out of this world. He then got on his knees, still holding my cock, massaging it lovingly. He took my hand and slipped my fingers in his mouth, just as he had my erection. He sucked hard and drenched them in his saliva, before he parted his legs and pushed my hand into the depths of his body. I started to move my fingers, knowing just what to do to tease him and torment him.

"I hope you don't mind that I watched porn. I just wanted to have a better idea of what I'm doing," he said, his words being lost to sharp moans.

"I don't mind at all," I said, grinning as he squeezed my cock while I touched a sensitive part of him. I rubbed him over and over again, feeling him shudder under the power of my fingers. It was such a glorious feeling to know that I literally had him in the palm of my hand, and I was only just beginning. I watched his body roll forward as he threatened to lose control of himself. It was luscious and gorgeous and I needed him badly. I was throbbing so hard I could feel myself primed to explode. Every muscle in my body was tensed. My skin was flushed with heat. My mind was focused on him and there was nothing I could do except to have him.

"Get on me," I ordered, my words rasping and harsh. He obeyed immediately.

He swung his legs over mine, straddling me. My hands fell to his waist and waited as he lowered himself onto me. He reached down, steadying me. I felt his tightness. He gasped and winced. There was no pleasure without a little bit of a pain. I felt the warmth as he stretched to accommodate me, and then we were one. A hazy grin broadened on my face as I relaxed into the sensations of it all. He leaned back and showed me the beauty of his naked body as he rolled back and forth, curling his hips. I held onto his waist as the bed creaked underneath us and the world tumbled all around me. I craned my neck back. We were both moaning as we were caught in the ecstasy of the moment, and our breaths surged through the air and became one with each other. Sweat trickled down and sizzled, pooling on me. He lunged forward and fell upon me, kissing me passionately. Our hands found each other and clasped tightly together as we battled and wrestled with our passion, our strength meeting each other. His body pressed into mine and I loved feeling the weight of him upon me. He slowed his motion and I took over, drilling myself into him, my hips moving like pistons as I cradled his body close to mine. His mouth was wide open and gasps poured out of him.

"I'm coming," he whispered. It didn't make me stop. I wanted to feel him come. I wanted to feel the pulsing surge of warmth explode over me and then it happened and, oh fuck, it was so fucking good. It came flooding over my stomach, bursting in a hot jet like a dam had just exploded. The moment I felt that warmth on my skin I came too, my body jerking wildly. I clung onto him tightly as I released everything I had inside him, and within moments we were breathless and spent.

He rolled off me and we both stared at the ceiling. Sweat glistened upon our chests. His lust simmered on my chest. I wasn't ready to move just yet. I wanted to enjoy the feeling of his pleasure upon me. My heart hammered and our chests were heaving. I rolled my head to the side and looked at this man beside me. He had once been my friend, then my enemy, and now he was my lover. I was glad I had sought him out because I knew this was going to be something wonderful. We were opposites in so many ways, but that was a good thing because it meant we complemented each other. All my missing pieces were in him, and I hoped that the same was true for him as well. I leaned in and kissed him softly, wanting to promise the world to him. For now I was just content to promise my heart.

Epilogue

Finn

About six months later...

I held a balloon as we walked through the hospital.

"I can't believe this day is finally here," Liam said.

"Me neither. It's really whizzed by," I replied. The last nine months had seen great changes in our lives. It hadn't taken long for me to move out of home and start living with Liam. We had picked up right where we had left off as kids, although we were older and wiser and now could fuck each other whenever we wanted. Dad wasn't too pleased at first, but I think he knew it wasn't doing me any good to be at home. After the reports came out about the beating that Liam had suffered Dad really had no choice but to accept that Liam was a good guy. It had taken some time, but they had finally reached a point where they could be civil with each other. I wasn't sure that it was going to be anything more than that, but hey, I'll take what I can get. It was better than them fighting at any rate.

I had gotten to know Liam's friends as well. It had been a tough time. They all had to recover from some things, and Linda had been forced to do community service and attend anger management. I didn't know her as well as Tess or Bailey. Everyone had come to Tess's side for the baby's birth. She had decided to keep it even though Hank didn't want to be a part of her life. It was his loss, she said. I happened to agree with her. I thought that one day Hank was going to wonder about his child and wish that he had been a part of its life.

The mistakes of youth were often so hard to correct.

We walked into the ward and saw Tess in bed. She looked pale and tired, but also happy. Her baby was in a crib beside her, close to the bed. Tess raised a finger to her lips, indicating that we should be quiet. Liam kissed her on the forehead while I smiled and tied the balloon to a chair. We looked at the little girl in the crib. She was impossibly small.

She shared her mother's complexion. Her nose was a button and she was just about the cutest thing I had ever seen.

"I think he's in love," Liam chuckled as he looked at me.

"She's going to be a heartbreaker alright. Everyone has the same reaction," Tess said, smiling.

"What's her name?" I asked.

"Leah. It was the closest sounding thing to Liam I could think of for a girl," Tess said. I smiled. Liam had no idea this had been going to happen.

"Wait, you named her after me?" he asked.

Tess reached out and took his hand. "You stood by me when I needed you. You got beaten up for me, even though I asked you not to, I might add. Leah may not have a father in her life, but she's going to need father figures, and I can't think of any better than you. You're my best friend Liam. Of course I was going to name her after you. She just made it more complicated by being a girl."

"I don't know what to say," Liam replied. I walked over to him and put my arm around his shoulder. I kissed him on the cheek and hugged him.

"Just say thanks," I said.

"Thanks," Liam replied, and we all laughed. We pulled up a chair and spoke to Tess about what had happened. She said that her family was taking a break. Liam asked if Hank had been in touch. Tess shook her head. I remarked that she must have been angry at him, but she denied this.

"You know, I was angry at him at first, but then when Leah was born I just felt sorry for him. There are so many things that he's going to have to miss out on because he can't stand up to his parents, and I just think that's really sad."

I asked her if she would ever consider allowing Leah to meet him if he reached out later on down the line. She said she was going to cross that bridge when they came to it. It wasn't long before Bailey arrived.

Things had stopped being awkward between her and Liam ever since they had both suffered at the hands of Bobby. The college had tried to cover it up, but too many people knew about it, and we weren't going to let them. The players had all been disciplined and were no longer able to play. It seemed as though the curse of that rival game was still going strong, it was just that the tables had turned and it was the Cavaliers who were suffering now.

We had to leave Tess and Leah a little early because we had a dinner date. It was an important night for us because it was the first night where our parents were going to see each other since dad had demanded them to leave. I wasn't sure how it was going to go and I needed to have another talk with dad to make sure that he was on his best behavior. However, I figured that if Liam and I could turn from enemies to lovers then perhaps our parents could become friends. Stranger things had happened after all.

*****

Enjoy what you read? Please leave a review. Thanks!

Don't miss out!

Visit the website below and you can sign up to receive emails whenever Van Cole publishes a new book. There's no charge and no obligation.

https://books2read.com/r/B-A-RTRV-JYGMC

Connecting independent readers to independent writers.

Did you love *Going Offside*? Then you should read *Triple Threat*[1] by Van Cole!

Hot new player Mats does more than just score goals.Arrogant, ambitious and good looking, he thrives on attention.And he just loves teasing team star, Keir.Keir is a ladies' man.He likes women.And he lives to party.So how does he wake up, unexpectedly married to someone he doesn't even like?But Mats knows how to push the right buttons.Before long, Keir is putty in his hands.And he's not the only one.Because there is a third person in this marriage – Keir's friend Finn.However, Keir is desperate to keep their mutual arrangement to himself.Unfortunately, life has other ideas and keeps thrusting him and his new husband into the spotlight.The attention which Mats craves so

---

1. https://books2read.com/u/4ARQV0

2. https://books2read.com/u/4ARQV0

much.Does Mats really have feelings for Keir and Finn, or is he just using them?Can three be the magic number in this hot romance?

Also by Van Cole

3 Man Huddle: MMM Best Friend Romance
His Alpha Wolf: Gay First Time Romance
A Dragon's Miracle: Gay Dragon MPREG Romance
Double-Teamed: MMM First Time Football Romance
His Football Star: Gay Second Chance Romance
Love In My Town: MM First Time Romance
Training A Hockey Star
Game Night
Double Shift
Take A Shot
Dear Professor
Getting Inked
Ninth Inning
Triple Threat
Seducing My Best Friend's Brother
My Protector
The Blueprint
Show Me The Way
End Zone
Matched To His Tiger
Love At First Puck
My Straight Boss
Falling For The Alpha
My Boss
On Thin Ice

Going Offside

www.ingramcontent.com/pod-product-compliance
Lightning Source LLC
Chambersburg PA
CBHW031431150726
47989CB00002B/901